Sunday, 4th

I keep having the same dream, night after night. The crops are burning in the fields, flames crackling, smoke blowing about in a freshening wind. And in the distance, the suburbs of London are also on fire, the roofs of the houses blazing bright red. I'm standing on the edge of a burning field. I look up at the sky which is full of smoke and leaping flames, and watch the rushing clouds that have turned crimson.

What does it all mean? I thought if I wrote it down I might make some sense of it, but I can't!

I'm writing this by candlelight because I dropped my torch and it's broken and I haven't got enough pocket money left to buy a new one. Harry's made this new rule that I've got to be asleep by ten, but I'm almost afraid to go to sleep now in case I have the dream again. Also, there's something else – there's a singe mark on my duvet which I'm sure wasn't there this morning. I know it's not the candle. It can't be. I always put it out.

Directly I've done that I make a note in the diary Dad gave me, just to be on the safe side, to prove I haven't fallen asleep. Like now. 11.30pm, May 4. Candle out.

So what's happening?

2

'Hello, mummy's boy!' jeered Tom, standing in the playground of St Corin's High School with his mates, grinning maliciously.

Sean knew that Tom hated him, but the feeling was mutual. Sean's new stepfather, Harry Chambers, was also Tom's father which made Tom his new stepbrother. Life was complicated enough. His parents' divorce had been awful, especially as his father had moved to Southampton. Now he was saddled with Tom as well. At least Tom didn't live with them, but *he* could see his father whenever he wanted to, which was more than Sean could.

Sean didn't get on with his stepfather mainly because Harry was trying too hard to win Sean's approval, but also because he kept making up new rules. The latest was ridiculous. Why did he have to be asleep by ten o'clock? No one could tell you to close your eyes and go to sleep. Not just like that. It wasn't fair.

'And how's mummy's boy this morning?' Tom goaded. 'Did she give you a big smacking kiss before you left home?'

Sean scowled. They had had a big row last weekend after Sean had accused Tom of cheating at chess. Sean's mum had intervened, and as a result, Tom had started to bully Sean at school. Although they were almost the same age, Tom was bigger and heavier with a shock of dark hair, while Sean was a skinny red-head.

Some people say that red-heads lose their cool fast, but Sean had a slow fuse. He took a long time to lose control, but when he did, he always went over the top.

'Mummy thinks Sean's good at chess, doesn't she? Mummy thinks Sean's such a clever boy.'

Sniggers rose as Tom's mates enjoyed the sarcastic teasing which Sean thought pathetically childish. But it was annoying too because it had happened several times before and always in front of what seemed to be an invited audience.

'A goodie, goodie boy,' continued Tom, shoving Sean hard in the chest.

For a moment Sean stayed where he was, rigid with tension. As he stared back at Tom, he noticed a faint crimson haze around Tom's shoulders.

With a howl of rage he launched himself at his enemy, fists flailing, and they both fell on to the hard tarmac of the playground, rolling and punching and kicking. They were soon surrounded by an ever-growing, cheering crowd, until Mrs Cage, the deputy head, pushed her way through.

'Stop that!' she commanded. 'Stop it at once.'

But neither Tom nor Sean wanted to stop, and it was several moments before Mrs Cage got her way. Slowly they pulled apart and staggered to their feet. Tom's nose was bleeding badly and Sean had the beginnings of a black eye.

Mrs Cage launched into a full attack. 'Don't either of you remember what the Head said at assembly yesterday? You're both in detention, but you'll see Mr Jenkins first.' She paused, sniffing the air. 'And where's that smell of burning coming from?'

There was a long silence.

Gasping for breath, Sean looked around him, noticing with satisfaction the tears of pain in Tom's eyes and the blood seeping into the handkerchief he was holding to his nose. Then, just over his shoulder, Sean saw flames breaking out in the long grass under the lab. Wasn't that someone hurriedly closing the window? The flames rose higher, crackling and roaring and soon they were leaping up against the side of the building.

Some of the students began to scream, moving back as the red tongues belched smoke as well as fire. Suddenly, Mr Dale, one of the science teachers, came running across the playground with a fire extinguisher. He aimed it at the flames, spurting foam over them until they died back, spluttering, leaving blackened grass and a charred window sill under the lab.

'Could have been nasty.' Mr Dale wiped his brow. 'How did that get going?'

'Who's been smoking?' Mrs Cage demanded.

'That fire couldn't have been started by a smouldering cigarette,' said Mr Dale. 'It's almost as if someone poured petrol on the grass.'

'Come on!' barked Mrs Cage. 'Who's responsible for this?'

There was general shuffling.

'What about you, Sean? Or you, Tom?'

'I didn't do it,' said Sean fiercely.

'Neither did I,' muttered Tom.

'Might have been an experiment, miss,' said a girl on the edge of the crowd.

'What kind of experiment?'

'We did it last week with Mr Burdett. Something to do with the sun's rays shining through glass and causing combustion.'

Mr Dale shook his head. 'The fire was far too fierce for that.'

'Well, whoever's responsible will be punished,' said Mrs Cage angrily. She turned grimly back to Sean and Tom. 'Follow me, you two.'

Keeping well away from each other, Sean and Tom trailed after Mrs Cage as she walked briskly ahead. Sean wondered again how the fire had started, but the more he thought about the incident, the more confused he became.

'I'll get you for this,' whispered Tom, dabbing tentatively at his nose.

'Try me. Just try me,' muttered Sean belligerently.

'Be quiet,' snapped Mrs Cage, going at such a pace they could hardly keep up with her. 'I don't want to hear another word out of either of you.'

Mr Jenkins, head teacher of St Corin's, was perceptive enough to recognise this was no ordinary fight as he gazed at the two dishevelled and battered figures standing sullenly on his office carpet.

'Thank you so much, Mrs Cage,' he said when she had finished her explanation, and she hurried out, looking disappointed that she was no longer needed.

'Of course you're stepbrothers now, aren't you?' said Mr Jenkins gently.

There was a long silence for neither Tom nor Sean wanted to admit to any such thing.

'Aren't you?' he repeated.

They both muttered that they were.

'Where's your father now, Sean?'

'In Southampton, sir.'

'How often do you see him?'

'Once a fortnight.'

'That's hard.'

'That's what the court said,' muttered Sean, trying not to sound upset. He was terrified of showing any emotion in front of Tom.

'Does the situation make you angry?'

Sean nodded, for at least he could admit to that.

'And what about you, Tom?'

'I see my dad when I want to.' He sounded triumphant.

'But you're officially living with your mother.'

'Yes.'

'He's got the best of the deal,' Sean mumbled.

'I haven't,' snapped Tom. 'I've got to see *you* when I go to my dad's.'

Mr Jenkins paused and then asked, 'Have *you* two even *tried* to get on?'

Tom muttered something and looked away. Sean didn't bother to reply.

'Well, Tom?' asked Mr Jenkins quietly.

'I've tried, but I just don't like him.'

'Why not?'

'I don't know.'

'You must do.'

'He's a wimp,' said Tom vaguely.

'Wimps don't get into fights. So where did you get that bloody nose?'

Tom looked down at the floor and said nothing.

'What about you, Sean? Do you try to get on with Tom?'

'He's too mouthy.'

The conversation, such as it was, ground to a halt and Mr Jenkins sighed.

'You're in a very difficult position, both of you. You've just got to try and get on with each other. 'As for now, I'm going to put you in detention, but I'm not going to take any further action.'

There was a hostile silence which seemed to Sean to go on for a very long time.

'So if *I'm* not going to take any further action, *you've* certainly got to.'

Neither Tom nor Sean spoke.

'So what are you going to do? Or would you prefer me to suspend you for fighting?'

That was the last thing either of them wanted.

Mum would go bananas, thought Sean. He was the first to speak. 'I'll try, sir.'

'What about you, Tom?'

'You're not going to make us shake hands, are you, sir?' Tom asked.

'I just want you to promise that you'll try and get on in a stressful situation.'

'OK, I'll try to,' he muttered.

'But how much effort are you both going to put in?' asked Mr Jenkins.

Sean risked a glance at Tom and saw that he had a funny sort of smile on his face. He wondered what it meant. Was Tom laughing at him? A sudden wave of rage swept through him. The whole situation was totally unfair. Tom could drop by and see his father whenever he wanted, but he had to wait a fortnight to see his. OK, he could phone him, but Horrible Harry, as he secretly called his stepfather, was always complaining about the bill.

Sean's rage increased. He wanted his dad and he wanted him now. They had done everything together. Gone fishing, played snooker, watched TV. Most important of all, Sean was a cross-country runner like his dad and they had run together and trained together. Now they couldn't do that any more. He stared at the carpet, consumed with anger.

Suddenly Sean smelt burning and looked around for its source. But he couldn't see anything. Maybe it was his imagination.

'Well?' asked Mr Jenkins impatiently. 'Have you *both* lost the power of speech?'

Sean looked up. Catching sight of Tom's silly smile, he felt an uncontrollable surge of rage, and without stopping to think, he slapped him as hard as he could round the face.

Tom staggered back, a great red weal on his cheek. Sean stood waiting for him to retaliate, but Tom just gazed at him in amazement, unable to really believe what had just happened. Even Mr Jenkins seemed at a loss for words, staring silently from one to the other. A clock chimed, a faint burst of off-key singing came from the music block and cheering from a classroom was abruptly terminated by a shouting teacher.

Suddenly Mr Jenkins came back to life again.

'What on earth did you do that for?' he snapped, 'I'm going to ring your mother and have you suspended.'

Instantly the feeling of power drained away, to be replaced by panic. 'Please don't, Mr Jenkins.' Sean knew he sounded about five years old and he could see that Tom was grinning again. Maybe he reckoned it was worth a slap to see Sean completely humiliated.

'You can't deliberately assault another pupil in my office and expect to get away with it, can you?'

'No, sir.'

Tom was rubbing his cheek now, no doubt pretending that the pain was greater than it was.

3

Tuesday, 6th. Lunchtime.

What a morning - I've been suspended! I don't usually fight, but in Tom's case I enjoyed trying to hurt him. I've never been so angry in my life. It's not just because he taunted me, it's because he's Harry's son. Mind you, I don't know what came over me in Jerkins's office - I just had this overwhelming urge to hit him combined with a real feeling of power. I've never felt like that before.

Over the last year I've felt as though I was taking everything that was dished out to me. Like I was a punch-bag and there was nothing I could do. I couldn't change the way Dad left Mum. I couldn't change her loneliness. I couldn't change her meeting Harry. I've always sat back and taken whatever life's dumped on me. But not any more. I'm going to take control of my life...

PS. That fire at school was really weird - it seemed to start from nothing.

Sean walked slowly home. It was just after half past twelve, and the suburban street seemed quiet and rather strange. Then he realised he had rarely been here at this time before. The familiar neighbourhood was like a foreign country, and everything looked alien, as if the lunch-time feel of the shops was quite different from tea-time. Of course, in reality, the shops and fire station, post box and zebra crossing, bus shelter and garage were exactly the same as they had always been.

Sean dawdled along the street, peering into shop windows, delaying the inevitable showdown. He knew Mum would be furious when he got home. Like Sean, his mother had a slow fuse but when she blew she really blew. He didn't really care what Harry would say, and as for Dad he'd phone him and explain.

Although Sean knew he was in big trouble, he was pleased he had confronted Tom. The fight, the slapping, seemed not only important but justified. After a while, however, the feeling of importance faded, for Sean knew that slapping Tom in front of Mr Jenkins had been incredibly stupid. He had just been so angry he had completely lost it.

The last time Sean had felt a surge of fury like this had been when his father had left for

Southampton. He had been on his own in the sitting room, and Mum had been out. Sean had pummelled the cushions, kicked the sofa, even punched at himself in his grief and loss and misery. Since then Sean had managed to keep his temper under control, but today it had broken out again like a raging demon.

'How *could* you do it? Fighting with Tom and then slapping him in front of Mr Jenkins?'

Mum was standing behind the kitchen table, her face pale and drawn. But instead of losing her own temper, she simply looked depressed.

Mrs Fields was tall and skinny like her son, and had long auburn hair that reached halfway down her shoulders. Sean loved her very much and hated upsetting her.

'I never thought you'd get violent. Just look at that eye of yours.'

'Tom was winding me up.'

'How?'

'It doesn't matter.'

His mother gazed at him, forgetting to be cross. 'I know it's been difficult for you. What with me and Dad splitting up –'

Sean winced. His father was a taboo subject.

Mum hardly ever mentioned his name and Harry never mentioned him at all. This was the first time she had referred to him in a very long time and although Sean desperately wanted to talk to her about Dad, now was not the time.

'I'm going to phone him,' he said. 'Tell him what happened.'

His mother ignored the comment, almost as if Sean hadn't spoken. 'You'll have to apologise to Tom. You realise that, don't you?'

'No,' snapped Sean. 'I'm not going to. Not ever.' He got up, ran into the hall and picked up the phone.

'Your father will still be at work,' she called after him.

Sean ignored her, and angrily punched in the number. He waited for a long time before crashing down the phone. He felt a fool. Of course Dad would be at work. Sean thumped his way up the stairs.

'I want to bathe that eye,' Mum called.

'No way.'

'What about some lunch?'

'I'm not hungry.'

'So what are you going to do?'

'None of your business.' Sean stamped into his

bedroom, slammed the door shut and threw himself on his bed, lying on his back and kicking off his school shoes. He had never felt so completely drained and, for a moment, the room looked very strange. The walls bulged and seemed to be made of plasticine. His fishing and cross-country posters were at odd angles and his computer looked like a mound of jelly. But in a second the room was completely normal again. Perhaps his black eye had affected his vision? Suppose he was going blind? He could sue Tom for thousands of pounds. He could…

Sean drifted into exhausted sleep and began to dream that he was standing on the edge of the field again, but this time the stubble was blackened. The flames had burnt themselves out, and when he gazed at the horizon the city was in ruins.

Then Sean heard a sort of scrunching sound and turned to see Tom stumbling towards him through the debris. He was wearing a football shirt and laughing maliciously, his expression full of loathing. A thin trickle of blood ran from his nose and as he came nearer, Sean saw he was pointing at a badge on his shirt which was embroidered with the word 'Southampton'.

'That's where Daddy is, isn't it? In Southampton.

That's hundreds and hundreds of miles away, isn't it, Sean? Much too far to go and visit.' Tom began to chant a nursery rhyme:

'Bye, baby bunting,
Daddy's gone a-hunting.
Gone to get a rabbit skin
To wrap the baby bunting in.'

As Sean's rage welled up inside him, flames rose from the ashes, engulfing his enemy, burning Tom to a crisp.

Sean woke with a start, sweating and afraid. He had always been afraid of fire, ever since he had seen a forest alight one very hot summer. He and Dad and Mum had been in no danger, but the road through the forest had been closed by the fire brigade and Dad had turned and driven back, trying to find another way around.

Sean had watched the blaze from the back window of the car. The flames leapt up the trees like vicious red snakes, licking at the trunks, branches and leaves, turning everything black and bringing the giant limbs crashing down into a deadly dark red crackling inferno. Sean could remember the whole thing as if it were yesterday.

Sean sat up to see late afternoon sunshine

filtering through the half-open window. He could hear dogs barking and the shouts of young children playing. As his nightmare began to fade, however, he saw that there was another singe mark on his duvet.

Immediately panic filled him. Then he wondered if Harry had sneaked into his room while he was at school. Maybe he'd been snooping around, puffing away at his fag, and had dropped hot ash on his duvet. He wouldn't put it past him.

Suddenly there was a loud knock on the door.

'Who is it?'

'Do you want some tea? I've done corned-beef fritters.' His mother sounded as exhausted as he was.

Pangs of hunger made Sean want to get up immediately and run downstairs, until he remembered his stepfather.

'Is Harry in?'

'Just.'

'Does he know what happened?'

'We're having a chat about it all.'

Now there was bound to be trouble.

'Come on, love,' said Mum loudly and brightly through the door. 'Nothing to be afraid of.'

'I'm not,' snarled Sean. He went over to the

mirror, and stared at his reflection. His eye had turned a disquieting mauve colour and had swollen up badly. A sudden onrush of self-pity almost swamped him. If only Dad hadn't gone away, thought Sean, none of this would ever have happened.

4

Mum and Harry are waiting for me downstairs, but I'd rather stay up here. I don't want to have to explain about the fight with Tom. Besides, there are still so many unanswered questions in my head. Was there really a burning smell in Mr Jenkins's office? Why was I the only one who could smell it? I don't understand what's happening and I feel really afraid. I keep thinking about the burning city in my dreams and the burning grass at school today...are they connected? And what about my singed duvet? Is that connected too?

Sean sat tensely at the table, eating his corned-beef fritters, wondering what was going to happen. His stepfather was large and well-built, like Tom, and his black hair gleamed with gel. But underneath his confident, well-polished exterior, Sean had always sensed a yearning to be liked that he had deliberately ignored. He had never been prepared to give Harry a chance.

'That's quite an eye you've got.'

'Tom got a bloody nose,' said Sean truculently.

'Fair enough. You had a scrap. I can understand that. It's not easy for either of you.' Harry cleared his throat. 'But why did you slap him in front of Mr Jenkins? Wasn't that a bit cowardly? You knew he couldn't hit you back.'

Mum looked down at her plate, as if she had temporarily handed over responsibility to Harry. Sean's anger began to simmer, but he was determined not to allow himself to be provoked.

'Well, he couldn't, could he?' Harry persisted after a long silence.

'Why not?' Sean was sullen.

'Maybe he had too much respect.'

Sean looked at Harry with contempt. How could Mum have ever fancied him, he wondered, he wasn't a patch on Dad. Then he had to remind himself that Dad had gone off with someone else. Not for long, because it didn't work out, but he had never come back and was now living in Southampton on his own. Harry was the manager of a local supermarket where Mum worked part-time, and when his wife had kicked him out they had started seeing each other. And now they were married. It was all terribly permanent.

'Respect for who?'

'Mr Jenkins, of course.'

'He was winding me up.'

'Who? Mr Jenkins?' Harry smiled at his feeble joke. Sean shook his head and scowled.

'Tom was winding me up.'

'You should have backed off.'

'Why?' Sean was surly, refusing to catch his mother's eye.

'That's the way to deal with a wind-up. I get enough of that at work, and what do I do? I back off.'

Sean's anger was suddenly at boiling point. 'Well, you would, wouldn't you?' he said angrily.

His stepfather's smile disappeared and Mum looked down at her plate again.

'What did you say to me?' demanded Harry.

'Honestly, Sean,' said Mum sadly. 'There's no need to be rude.'

'I'm waiting for an explanation,' said Harry. His stepfather looked more hurt than offended, but Sean didn't want to think about Harry's feelings. He got to his feet, anger boiling over into red-hot rage.

'Well you won't get one. You're not my dad. I don't have to explain anything to *you*.'

'Sean!' gasped Mum, her face white with shock.

'I'm not taking this,' said Harry jumping to his feet.

'Neither am I.' Sean walked to the door.

'Where do you think you're going?'

'To phone Dad.'

'I forbid you to leave this room,' Harry shouted pompously. 'I won't allow it!'

'You and whose army?' demanded Sean as he pulled open the door.

'Your father's no example, is he?' Harry goaded.

'*What?*'

'Harry,' intervened Mum. 'Let him go. Don't make a thing of it. I want to see your eye, Sean.'

But Sean only had ears for Harry. '*What* did you say?' he yelled.

'I said your father's no example. Look at the way he treated your mother.'

Harry's figure seemed to be outlined in a kind of crimson haze and Sean was sure he could smell burning. He strode back to the table, picked up an open bottle of brown sauce and taking slow and careful aim he shook the contents all over his stepfather's white shirt. As he did so the TV set suddenly came on, its sound blasting out so loudly that their ears hurt. For a moment they all hesitated, surprised at what had happened. Then Sean saw the remote control had fallen to the floor. The TV must have switched itself on.

Harry grabbed the control, switched off the TV and then suddenly dropped the control on the floor.

'It's hot,' he shouted, looking at the red marks on his fingers.

Seeing a chance to escape, Sean ran out into the hall and slammed the front door behind him.

He jogged through the streets of the estate, the sun low on the twilit horizon, feeling more angry and lonely than he had ever felt before.

Sean needed to speak to his father and hear his reassuring voice telling him they'd see it through together. But see what through, he wondered. Life? The future? What on earth *could* they see through together now?

Sean reached the phone box next door to the used car lot that garishly traded as SID'S SUPER SALES. But the phone had been vandalised. His rage increased and he banged down the receiver as hard as he could, feeling the same surge of power that he had experienced in Mr Jenkins's office.

Suddenly a series of vivid flashes lit up the

phone box in an unearthly light, and peering through the smudged, dirty glass, Sean was amazed to see a dazzling display of synchronised hazard lights – perhaps this was some kind of new sales gimmick for Sid's used car lot. At the same time the interior of the telephone box bent out of shape and then reformed.

Sean gasped, horrified at what was happening, and a cold clutch of fear seized the pit of his stomach. It must be his eye. Something terrible had happened to his eye – and it was all Tom's fault.

Outside, passers-by were stopping to look, and Sid ran out of his battered caravan, hurrying between the rows of his gaudily price-stickered cars, desperately trying to stop the light show.

Puzzled, Sean pushed open the door of the phone box and was almost blinded by the flashing hazard lights. He stood and stared and then started to head for the gathering crowd, but the road seemed distorted, out of focus, and a sense of panic coursed through him again. What was happening? Why did things keep going out of shape? Then he smelt burning.

He crossed the road, and saw a thin wisp of smoke drifting from a Vauxhall at the front of the lot. But it disappeared as soon as the lights stopped flashing.

'I don't get it,' said Sid in his down-at-heel sports jacket and grubby flannels. 'I've never seen anything like that happen before. I mean, it's as if there's an electrical charge in the air. Maybe we're heading for a storm.'

Sean gazed at the huge sign illuminated by coloured lights.

SID'S SUPER SALES
DE LUXE MOTORS FOR BARGAIN PRICES

Most of the bulbs were missing, and as he stared up at them, the lights flickered slightly and then a bulb popped and fell to the ground, smashing on the concrete. Sean felt drained, as if all his strength had left him.

'Must be the alarms,' said someone.

'Alarms?' Sid laughed derisively. 'This lot don't have alarms.'

'Something triggered 'em off. Might be some kind of freak circuit.'

Sid looked at the passer-by irritably. 'You're an electrician then, are you?'

'I'm a double-glazing salesman. I suppose you don't –'

'No,' said Sid. 'I don't. Now push off. All I know is that something, or someone, has been interfering with my property.'

He went back to his caravan and banged the door.

The smell of burning lingered in the air and Sean decided to go home. He would feel safer there, whatever the consequences he would have to face.

With a sickening lurch, Sean suddenly remembered that he hadn't phoned his father. How *could* he have forgotten. Well, he'd make the call from home. Why should he be forced to ring Dad from a call box?

5

'Where have you been?' Harry didn't sound angry. In fact, he looked a bit pathetic as he stood hesitantly on the doorstep in his tracksuit, almost as if he had become afraid of his stepson.

'I went to call Dad, but the phone's out of order in that box up the road,' lied Sean.

'Your mother's out of her mind with worry.'

Sean said nothing, wondering what was going to happen next.

'Tom called.'

'Yeah?'

'You were right. He said he *had* been winding you up. I think Tom's trying to made amends.' Harry sounded wary.

'Really?'

'You ruined my shirt,' he said reproachfully. 'You've got a temper just like your mother's.'

'I'm sorry.' Sean decided to be repentant, surprised that his stepfather was being so tolerant.

'Your mum's really upset. She's been trying to get the stain out of the carpet. Funny about that red-hot remote control. I burnt my fingers. Not badly though –'

Sean frowned but said nothing.

'Well come on in. Your eye needs attention.'

'I want to phone Dad.' He felt as if he had betrayed his father and wondered again how he could possibly have forgotten to ring.

'Do it here.'

Sean wondered if he should apologise again, but decided against it.

'All right,' he replied grudgingly.

'I want us to get on better,' said Harry. 'Can't we both try harder?'

Harry sounded just like Mr Jenkins, but Sean felt he had to say something reasonable, just for Mum's sake, so he mumbled and nodded.

'We're not making a very good job of it so far, are we?'

'No.'

'Tom's sorry.'

'Yeah.'

'And Mr Jenkins phoned again –'

'What about?'

'He wants you to go back to school tomorrow.'

'He's changed his mind?'

'We had a chat.'

'What about?'

But Harry didn't say, just hurried on to the result

of the conversation. 'Mr Jenkins didn't think there was any point in you sitting around at home, doing nothing. He thought that if you're really sorry, you'd better go back to school again.' Harry paused and then sighed as Sean made no reply. 'So are you sorry?'

'Yes,' he said grudgingly.

'You're going to make it up with Tom?'

'I'll try.'

'I do understand how difficult this is. It's stressful for all of us.'

As he passed Harry in the hallway, Sean prayed he wouldn't attempt to put an arm round his shoulders. Fortunately he didn't, but Sean still felt a bitter resentment. It was his dad who should have been talking to Mr Jenkins, not Harry who was constantly trying to take over, get in with him, rub Dad out. The yearning for his father welled up in Sean yet again, but much more forcefully this time, and the combination of rage and pain was unbearable. As far as he was concerned, Mum seemed to have forgotten Dad, and Harry and Tom were infiltrators, trying to conquer Sean, to reduce him to nothing.

Mum was down on her knees, scrubbing the carpet.

'I'm sorry,' said Sean, but this time with more

sincerity. She was very house-proud and home had always meant everything to her. Since Dad had left, she regularly and obsessively cleaned the house from top to bottom each week.

'I think the stain's coming out,' she said, sitting up and wiping the sweat from her forehead. 'After a bit of a struggle.'

Sean knew he should stay and talk to her, offer to help, but first he had something he needed to do. 'I'm going to phone Dad.'

'Let me have a go at that eye first,' said his mother, sounding hurt.

But Sean was already running up the stairs to the extension on the landing.

6

I'm waiting for Harry to get off the phone
so I can ring Dad. Dad is the one person I
can always rely on to stay calm. Mum's
temper is almost as bad as mine - once
she gets going. OK, so Dad made a bad
mistake, but we all make mistakes.
Couldn't Mum see that? Anyway, he's on his
own again now. So why does he have to live
in Southampton?

If only he could get a job in Bostock,
Dad could be near me then.

I hope he can reassure me about all
the weird things that have been going on.

'Dad?'

'Sean?'

'Are you OK?' Sean was so pleased to hear his
father's voice that he almost burst into tears.

'What's up?'

'Nothing.'

'Of course there is. I can always tell.'

'I had a bit of a run-in with Tom.'

'What do you mean, a run-in?'

'A fight.'

'Who won?'

'I'm not sure. But then I slapped him in front of Mr Jenkins.'

'Oh dear.' His father sounded slightly bemused but not particularly shocked. 'Why did you do that?'

'I hate him. He winds me up.'

'What happened?'

'I got sent home, but I can go back tomorrow.'

'What about Tom?'

'He's sorry. Apparently.'

'Are you going to say sorry?'

'I might... Dad –'

'Yes?'

'I keep having these dreams.'

'What dreams?'

'There are crops burning in a field. And a city alight with flames. And I keep smelling burning when I'm awake. Do you remember that forest fire we almost drove through? I keep thinking about it.'

'You're going through a lot of stress right now –' his father began, and Sean wondered how many more adults were going to say that to him. What's more, Dad sounded horribly like a stranger – even the tone of his voice was different. It was as if he was dead and there was an impostor on the line. But when he thought about it, the impostor seemed to have been there for some time. Nowadays the weekends when Sean *did* see his father seemed oddly forced, as if Dad was only the shadow of the man he used to be.

'Only a few days to go and you'll be coming down to Southampton. We'll have a talk then.'

Why couldn't Dad drive up and see him, Sean thought miserably. It wasn't that far on the motorway.

'I had a row with Harry and chucked some sauce over him.'

'That wasn't very clever.' Dad sounded as if he didn't care either way. Was he yawning?

'I lost my temper.'

'That temper of yours. Your Mum's got it too. Did Tom hurt you?' He suddenly sounded more protective, but Sean still found him oddly distant.

'I got a black eye.'

'Is it painful?'

Black eyes usually are, thought Sean savagely. 'Mum's going to bathe it,' he replied abruptly.

'What did you give Tom?' His father sounded competitive and Sean felt a stab of irritation. Adults could be worse than kids, always wanting to score points off each other in a snide sort of way. However much he loved Dad, however much he longed to see him, Sean suddenly wanted to ring off and give his mother a chance to bathe his eye which was really hurting now.

'He got a bloody nose.'

'Good for you.'

'Dad – I've got to go.'

'OK. See you soon.'

'Great!'

A few moments later, Sean put down the phone and went downstairs. His head ached and his eye thudded with pain. He had the unsettling feeling that the father he had known so well and loved so much no longer existed. When he opened the kitchen door, Mum and Harry were sitting at the table, drinking coffee.

'There you are,' said Mum. 'Let's have a go at that eye.' She sounded too eager.

Nothing felt right any more, Sean thought miserably. Dad didn't care enough and Mum was over-compensating. No wonder he sometimes saw the world out of shape. 'Don't you want to know how Dad is?' he asked.

'How is he?' She sounded like an automaton.

'OK.'

'That's fine then.' Now she was brisk. 'Sit down and I'll bathe that eye.'

'Will it be painful?'

'Maybe a bit.'

Sean couldn't stand any more pain tonight. 'Why don't you bathe it in the morning?'

'Why don't you shut up and sit down and let me help you.' There was a sudden sharp edge to her voice and Sean realised his mother was on the verge of losing her own temper.

After his mother had finished and Sean had waited for Harry to go and collect the evening paper from the doormat, he said, 'My sight's gone a bit weird.'

She was immediately concerned. 'What do you mean?'

'It's kind of distorted.'

Mum looked closely into his eyes, trying to see what was wrong, and when Harry came back she snapped at him, 'Now look what your son's gone and done.'

'What's up?'

'Sean says he's got distorted vision. Why didn't you tell me before?'

'It doesn't happen all the time. Only occasionally. It's as if everything's bending.'

Harry got in first, anxious to take the initiative and show how decisive he could be. 'I think he should go to the doctor tomorrow morning.'

Sean scowled.

'But that'll mean he'll miss more school.'

'We have to be sure he's OK.'

Now they were talking about him as if he wasn't there and Sean wanted to go up to his room, lie on the bed and think about life as it had been.

'I'm going to bed, Mum. I'm tired.'

'Have you done your homework?' she asked wearily.

'Yes.'

'Are you sure?'

Sean nodded. He hadn't of course, but wasn't prepared to tell her. He would have to try and scribble it out tomorrow morning.

'I'll ring the doctor first thing in the morning.'

'Sweet dreams,' said Harry as Sean went up to bed.

Sean started, for by some awful coincidence that was exactly what Dad had often said. Even Mum looked thrown. Was Harry *becoming* Dad? And had Dad already become somebody else?

7

Tuesday, 6th

It's 3.00am and I've just had another
nightmare. This time I dreamt about
Harry. He was wearing a green dressing
gown and kept bowling cricket balls at me
while I stood at the wicket with nothing to
protect me, not even a bat in my hand,
unable to move as the hard leather
thumped me in the face and chest. I kept
telling him to stop, but Harry only grinned.
'They're good for you,' he said. 'You need
thumping.'
What does it all mean?
And I can smell burning again. It's getting
stronger. I'll have to investigate...

Sean jumped out of bed, switched on the light,
opened the door and stood at the top of the stairs.
With sudden shock he realised he could see a little
plume of smoke drifting across the hall from the
kitchen.

Panic swept over him as he ran down the stairs and

coughed as the smoke in the hall caught at the back of his throat. Cautiously, he opened the kitchen door and a dense toxic cloud billowed out, making him cough even harder.

Sean froze as he saw the tongues of fire that were sliding like snakes over the hearthrug, growing larger all the time, their tips shooting up to the ceiling.

How could he feel so cold when the heat from the blaze was already scorching him?

Sean gave a cry of terror as one of the snake flames whipped towards him. Then the smoke thickened and he began to cough again. But Sean knew what he had to do. He knew he had to smother the red-hot flames now. If he didn't, they would curl around him, burning him to a dry, fleshless crisp. Suddenly, he half remembered a video he had seen at school about safety in the home. Damp towels. He had to get some damp towels.

Sean ran to the downstairs toilet, dragged a towel off the back of the door, hurried to the tap and soaked the thick material in the basin. He wrapped the wet towel round his mouth and nose and ran back into the kitchen. He wasn't wearing anything on his feet, and as he approached the blazing hearth rug he trod on some cinders and cried out in pain. But there was no time to lose. Hurriedly Sean searched through the drawers for tea towels and tablecloths, soaked them in the sink and threw them over the rug. The smoke immediately thickened but the flames hissed and died back a little.

Then he saw one of Harry's tracksuits hanging on the kitchen line and ruthlessly threw it on the spluttering fire. Once again, the smoke increased, but he clamped the wet towel over his face again, and with one hand awkwardly piled more clothes from the line on to the rug, desperately trying to smother the blaze completely. He did this again and again until there was no sign of even the smallest of flames – and no sign of any clothes on the line either. The smoke, however, was still thick, and when he was sure the fire was out Sean dashed to the windows and opened them wide, gasping for air.

Gradually the smoke began to clear until only a few strands were left, and although there was a filthy smell of burning, a pile of charred material and a mound of cindery debris where the rug had once been, there was little other damage. Sean was surprised and then proud that he had overcome his fear of fire and had been able to successfully defeat the snakes of red flame.

'What do you think you're doing?' Harry was standing in the doorway, wearing the green dressing gown he had worn in Sean's nightmare, his face twisted with fury. 'Trying to burn the house down? Look at the mess you've made in here. What are you? Some kind of psycho?'

Sean opened his mouth to explain, but Harry wouldn't let him get a word in.

'Wait a minute. Wasn't that my tracksuit?' Harry grabbed at the charred remains as Mum appeared in the doorway, looking totally bewildered. 'You deliberately set my tracksuit alight.'

Suddenly he hit Sean a glancing blow round the back of the head, and taken off-guard, Sean tripped over the burnt rug, and fell into the cindery mess.

'Can't you see what's happened, you raving idiot!' Mum yelled, recovering from her numbed silence and pushing Harry away, 'Sean was trying to put a fire out not start one.'

'Eh?'

'How dare you hit my son? How dare you! I don't care if he burnt every tracksuit you ever owned. He had to take everything else off the line as well. Can't you see what he was trying to do? There was a fire in here. Maybe I didn't turn the gas off properly. You know how heavily we both sleep. We could have been burnt alive in our beds if it hadn't been for Sean!'

Harry backed away, recoiling from the torrent of words, realising his mistake. Sean stared at the walls which suddenly looked as if they had melted in the heat and were drooping towards him, beginning to ooze mortar. He blinked and they were solid again. The chill began to creep back into his stomach. Could there be something seriously wrong with his eyesight?

'Why do you and your son enjoy hitting my boy?' Mum asked. The question gave Sean an immense feeling of satisfaction. He didn't mind being hit a dozen times if it meant that Harry and Tom would get into trouble. If only she would tell Harry to leave, force him to roam the streets in his green dressing gown. If that happened, Mum might even phone Dad and he'd drive up from Southampton, make amends and they would all live happily ever after.

Instead, Harry said with a sincerity that even Sean couldn't dispute, 'I've been an utter fool and

I'm very sorry.' He spoke slowly and sorrowfully. 'I completely misunderstood the situation.'

'You *wanted* to blame me,' said Sean, staring at the burnt mess of clothes and cinders.

Harry shook his head. 'I just got confused. I've been so worried about you and Tom, it's all been on my mind so much that I just jumped to the wrong conclusion and I'm deeply, deeply sorry. I don't know what to say.'

'You've said enough,' said Mum softening. To Sean's dismay, she went over and put her arms around Harry. It wasn't fair, she should have been putting her arms round him. Sean felt totally alone. Once again, Harry seemed to be in control, taking his mother's love away.

Sean was outraged. 'He hit me,' he yelled, trying not to lose his temper, staring blankly at them both.

'I'll leave you two alone and go back to bed,' said Harry. 'I don't expect you want me around after all this.' He glanced at Sean. 'I'm very sorry I hit you, Sean. I'm not a violent man. It was just the heat of the moment.'

The heat of the moment. The phrase leapt up like a flame in Sean's mind. It was as if his stepfather knew something. But what *was* there to know?

*

'You were very brave,' said Mum when Harry had gone. She handed Sean a steaming cup of hot chocolate and they sat down at the table, ignoring the mess on the floor. 'In fact, you were fantastic.'

Sean shrugged but said nothing. Hearing his mother's praise was like lying in the most beautifully warm bath after he had run cross-country. Then the moment was spoilt as he remembered how Mum had put her arms round Harry. 'It wasn't that difficult,' he said. 'I remembered to wrap a wet towel round my nose and mouth.' He began to explain and found that his mother was giving him all her attention, something Sean was sure she hadn't done for a long time. He wound up by saying, 'I'm sorry about your tablecloths and all that stuff on the line, Mum.'

'They don't matter. What matters is that we're all alive, thanks to you.'

'I'm sorry about throwing sauce at Harry too.' Sean felt as if he was going through some kind of penance, appeasing his guilt.

'I used to feel that kind of rage against your dad sometimes. I guess it's because we're both red-heads. We fire up.'

'I'll try to get on better with Tom.' Penance again.

'I expect he finds it difficult too.'

'Maybe I've been selfish.' Now he was just trying to get on good terms with her so that, together, they could better fight the enemy.

'I know Harry can be clumsy and insensitive. After all, that's probably why his wife –' She seemed to run out of words.

'Do you love him, Mum?'

'He's been very kind to me.'

Sean knew she wasn't answering honestly, but he didn't press her for he didn't really want to know what she felt about Harry. He was too afraid of what she might say.

'Do you still love Dad?' he asked hopefully, but his mother hurriedly returned to a safer topic.

'You threw brown sauce all over Harry and once I doused your father in red wine.' She paused again and then reached out over the table, taking Sean's hands in hers. 'So what are we going to do? How are we going to stop losing our tempers?'

'I don't know, Mum. But I'll try with Tom…unless he deliberately winds me up again. I can't take that.'

'Harry's a good man at heart. He really wants to

get on with you. In fact, he probably tries too hard.'
She got to her feet. 'I'll clean up and you go back to
bed. You've got school tomorrow, but I'll make an
appointment with the doctor first. Just to make sure
nothing's wrong with your eyesight. Although I'm
sure there isn't –'

Sean felt a rush of irritation. Did she think he'd
been making it all up? Suddenly he was swamped
by fatigue. 'It's been quite a night,' he said.

'You can say that again!'

His mother put her arms around him, just as she
had done with Harry. Sean went rigid. Suddenly he
could smell burning again.

8

I can hardly believe what's just happened - was the fire in the kitchen just a coincidence too?

I can't explain why, but I feel really uneasy - it seems like every time there's a fire, I'm right there in the thick of it. I wish I could talk to Dad instead of this diary. I keep reading his inscription on the first page.

> *To my dear son Sean*
> *From your father, with much love.*

I can hardly bear to read the words - I feel so alone without him. I've just done something really stupid. I've just re-read what I'd written about the burning field and the city. The description is so vivid it really unnerved me. I'll never get to sleep now.

'Where's Harry?' asked Sean at breakfast.

'He's not feeling very well,' said Mum. 'He's going to take the day off and have a sleep-in.' She smiled with vague affection and he couldn't work out whether it was for him or Harry. 'I've made an appointment with the doctor at 8.30. Then you can go straight on to school.'

Sean felt apprehensive at the mention of school. He didn't feel tired, despite his broken night, but he didn't want to go to school, not after his suspension, for everyone was bound to be asking him questions he didn't want to answer.

'Can't I stay at home? I'm scared my eyes might start to play tricks again.'

'Let the doctor decide that. I don't want the two of you here all day.' She spoke lightly with a half-smile, but Sean was immediately hurt. So she'd rather have Harry at home, would she? He knew when he wasn't wanted.

Sean felt a surge of jealous rage and then a kind of blackness. He closed his eyes and Harry's phrase – *The heat of the moment* – slid into his mind. With a start, Sean realised that he could smell burning again and as he opened his eyes flames were shooting out of the toaster. They were back. The snakes with tongues of fire were back. Perhaps he hadn't smothered them all last night. They'd been waiting all this time, just waiting to break out again. He'd never get rid of them. Never.

Once the toast had been burnt to a crisp, the flames died back and he and Mum gazed down at the blackened mess and then at each other. Sean saw that his mother was very shaken.

'What's happening to us?' she half whispered.

'It's an electrical fault,' he muttered. 'Just a coincidence.'

'Is it?'

'What else could it be?' Sean got up and switched off the toaster at the socket. 'I'm going to the doctor.'

'Sean –'

'Yes?'

'Be careful.'

'There's nothing wrong,' said Dr Page, sitting down behind her desk to write out a prescription. 'Your mother's done a good job bathing that eye, but I'm going to give you an antibiotic cream just in case of infection.'

'How come I had all that distorted vision?'

'Shock,' she said briskly. 'You don't get punched in the eye every day.' Dr Page smiled. 'In the old days you'd have put raw steak on it. Maybe some of those old remedies really do work.'

'You're quite sure there's nothing wrong?' Sean persisted.

'Absolutely. Obviously, you'll have slightly hazy vision in that eye because of the swelling, but it'll soon clear up.'

'Should I go to school?'

'Oh yes,' Dr Page replied casually. 'But try not to let anyone black the other one.' She laughed heartily and Sean gloomily left the surgery, feeling defeated.

It was a hot morning and Sean felt claustrophobic as he tried to stroll casually across the playground, but as he passed heads turned and he could sense that people were whispering about him. He soon discovered that the news of his fight with Tom had spread, and other pupils were looking at him with a new respect. Why should violence bring such acceptance, wondered Sean, but of course he knew why. He was now a force to be reckoned with.

'It's all over,' he kept telling them. 'There's nothing to say.'

But they persisted, determined to discover the cause of the fight, disappointed that he wasn't co-operating. Then, in the distance, Sean saw Tom kicking a ball around with his mates, and turned away, keen to avoid him. In fact he managed to avoid Tom all day, although this wasn't particularly difficult as he wasn't in any of his classes or his tutor group. Sean was determined not to make the first tentative move. He wanted Tom to take the initiative.

Then, just as Sean was going home, he heard his name being called and Tom hurried up, looking awkward and strained.

'I want to talk.'

'What about?'

'I'm sorry about your eye. Let's go to McDonald's. There's a special offer.'

'I haven't got any money.' Sean was immediately suspicious. Why was Tom being so generous? He sensed that Tom was forcing himself to be friendly.

'I'll treat you.'

'You can't do that –'

'Why not? Dad gave me some extra pocket money.'

Sean didn't want to be in Tom's debt, particularly if Harry was part of the conspiracy and had given him the extra funds, hoping to lure him into some kind of reconciliation. But Mum was right. They had to try and make a fresh start and he supposed it might as well be now. 'OK,' he said, 'but I can't be too long. I want to go running tonight. I'm sorry about slapping you in Jenkins's office,' said Sean quickly. 'I just lost my cool.'

'That's OK. You hungry?'

'I'm starving.'

'Let's go then.' There was an edge to Tom's voice that Sean didn't like.

Tom and Sean sat at a table in McDonald's with a couple of double cheeseburgers.

'What's the matter?' asked Tom, wolfing down his burger.

Sean was staring at the sachets of brown sauce on the table. They were exactly the same rich brown colour as the bottle he had chucked over Harry and he saw that Tom was looking at them too. Did he know what Sean had done to his father? Did he know about last night? The unanswered questions made him feel increasingly uneasy.

'I don't feel hungry any more.'

'Can I have yours?' asked Tom greedily.

Sean shoved it across, still wondering how much he knew.

'Dad phoned me first thing. Gather you had a bit of a fire last night.' Tom sounded tense.

'Yeah, only a small one. I don't think he felt too good this morning.'

'Just shock, really.'

'Did he tell you I threw a bottle of sauce over him?' Sean blurted out.

'What did you do that for?' Tom asked sharply.

'I lost my temper.'

'Your mum's got one too, hasn't she?' There was definitely a hard edge to Tom's voice now.

'What do you mean?'

'Your mum's got a temper,' Tom goaded.

'Your dad tell you that as well?'

'He might have done.'

'Did he, or didn't he?'

'He told me.'

'What did he say?'

'That your mum has a temper.' Tom was triumphant. He'd really wound up Sean this time.

'He shouldn't have told you,' Sean yelled angrily.

'Why?'

'It's not fair.'

'I'm his son.'

'That's his problem.'

'Don't start getting worked up again.' Tom was more cautious now. 'Remember who bought the burgers, even if you aren't hungry.' He opened a sachet of sauce. 'Can't we try to be friends?' Tom asked artificially.

Sean pushed back his chair and stood up.

'Where do you think you're going?'

'I've got to go home.'

'Don't you want to be friends?' said Tom, but there was a mocking tone to his voice. 'Don't go. I'll buy you a milk shake.'

'It's getting late.'

'What do you like? Chocolate? Banana? I'll –'

But Sean was already hurrying towards the door, knowing he had to get out before he lost his temper and something terrible happened.

'I've got to go. I can't be late.'

He was through the door in a minute, running down the street towards home.

The street seemed to have a slight red tinge and was gradually bending, becoming distorted. The shops were huddled, sinewy and twisting, wide and stretched out at the top, thin and narrow at the bottom. A lamp-post looked as if it was melting, the pavement was soft and spongy and the bus shelter had swollen up with huge concrete legs. Passers-by had long protruding noses and chins, their hands were enormous and their legs were either thin and stick-like or fat and waddling. The traffic was all kinds of weird shapes and sizes, with cars that had tiny bodies and huge tyres and trucks that had huge bodies and tiny cabins.

Sean blinked several times and the distortions vanished, but the red tinge had grown sharper and deeper and more crimson. His eye felt painful and it began to itch. Sean had to use all his self-control to avoid rubbing at it.

Suddenly all his problems seemed insurmountable and Sean wanted to hit out and hurt someone. For a moment his rage was completely uncontrollable and he kicked a lamp-post so hard that he wondered if he had broken his foot.

Sean hopped around, clutching at his trainer and groaning until he realised he was being watched with amusement by an older boy from school who he vaguely recognised as one of the heavies in Year Ten.

'That wasn't very clever, was it?'

All the rage in Sean suddenly died away and the crimson outline to the street faded to light red and then to nothing at all.

'Did you deliberately kick that lamp-post?'

'No,' snapped Sean bitterly. 'I was looking for a pillar box to kick. Made a bit of a mistake, didn't I?'

The boy looked at him blankly and then hurried on, loudly declaring, 'Right nutter, that one.'

Considering everything that had happened to him, Sean thought he was probably right, but the cold fear soon clutched at his stomach. What was happening to him? Was he really going mad? Or was there something badly wrong with his vision that the doctor had missed?

When he got home, Sean's anxiety about his eye was immediately replaced by a gathering anger as he remembered his conversation with Tom. How dare Harry tell Tom all about Mum's temper? How dare he!

Sean sat down on the sofa, punched the cushions a couple of times and then hurled one of them across the room. He flicked on the TV and tried to concentrate on a soap opera, and was just starting to relax a little when the picture disappeared.

Irritated, Sean switched it back on again. The screen came alive for a few seconds and then switched itself off. He flicked the control and the same thing happened, again and again until he felt like screaming.

'Mum?' he shouted.

'What is it?' she yelled from the kitchen.

'TV's on the blink.'

She came in, looking puzzled.

'It keeps switching itself off,' said Sean.

'What does?'

'The TV,' he said furiously. 'It won't work.'

'What do you expect me to do about it?' She grabbed the control. The screen flickered and then went blank. She tried again and again but all that happened was a slight flickering and then blankness yet again. 'I'll call the engineer.'

'When?'

'Look, Sean –'

'*When* are you going to call the engineer?'

'Don't shout at me!'

Suddenly the TV set came on at full blast, so deafening that the sound shook both of them and Mum looked down at the control, her face screwed up in pain. 'The thing's red-hot.' She dropped it on the ground and the set went blank. 'The same thing happened to Harry yesterday. I'm going to have to sort out the electrical equipment in this house. I need to have an electrician –'

'You must have turned up the volume,' snapped Sean.

'I didn't,' she shouted.

'You *must* have done –'

His mother turned to him, her eyes full of fury.

'Don't tell me what I did and didn't do,' she shouted.

'Don't lose your temper with me!' yelled Sean at the top of his voice.

Mum gingerly picked up the control and the TV sound was back at full blast but with the focus slipping, the picture rolling over.

'Turn down the volume,' shouted Sean.

'I have,' she retorted.

'Give me the control.' He snatched it out of her hand, and switched off the set.

There was a long, deep silence.

'I'm sorry,' said Mum. 'I just lost my –'

'Temper?'

She nodded, almost in tears.

'So did I,' said Sean, immediately contrite.

'I'll ring the engineer now.'

As she moved to the telephone, he said, 'I'm really sorry, Mum.'

'So am I. We're much of a muchness, you and I.'

He had always loved her phrase 'much of a

muchness'. It sounded like a comforting hug.

'By the way, Tom phoned.'

'Yes?'

'He wants you to call him after six.'

'OK.'

'You don't sound very keen.'

'Don't worry, I'll call him back.' Then a thought struck him. 'Wasn't Harry meant to be ill? I thought he was going to stay in bed all day.'

'He got restless and went in to work. Not a man for lying in bed, is Harry.' Unexpectedly she leant over and gave Sean a kiss.

He felt a rush of hope. He and Mum were getting close again. But how long would it last?

9

Well, I got through school without being suspended! The trip to McDonald's with Tom confused me though. I can't decide whether Tom's trying to be friends or if it's all an elaborate plot to get me. And why did he phone me? What does he want?

At least Mum and me are back on track. I want Mum to love <u>me</u>, not Harry. I want her love back. Every bit of it. Then maybe she won't have any left for Harry.

PS. There's something strange going on with the TV – it's as if it's got a will of its own – is that just another coincidence?

'What do you want?' asked Sean brusquely when he got through to Tom on the phone.

'Why did you run out?'

'I had to get home.'

'You really don't like being with me, do you?' Tom seemed oddly unsure of himself.

'I told you, I was late. I had to get home. So what do you want?'

'A favour.'

'What is it?'

'I want you to teach me to run.'

Sean was incredulous. 'Well, you put one foot in front of the other and slowly increase speed, making sure you don't trip over.'

'I'm serious.' He still sounded unsure.

'What do you want to run for? You're a football fanatic.'

'I want to do something a bit more challenging. Really push myself, maybe go in for a marathon.'

'That's a different kind of running.'

'I just need a few tips –'

Sean reluctantly relented. 'OK. I'll take you for a run in the park some time.'

'How about now?'

'*Now?*'

'I want to start right away.'

Sean was bewildered. Tom had never shown the slightest interest in cross-country running before, so why now? Maybe he really was trying to be friends.

'OK. I'll see you down there at seven.'

Still puzzled, Sean jogged down to the park, trying and failing to work out what was going on, still regarding Tom and Harry as the marauding enemy who were digging deeper into his life through a mysterious underground labyrinth of their own. Were they scenting victory, wanting to enslave him by worming their way into his affections in a variety of different ways? Maybe Tom's desire to learn to run was one of them.

Dimly, on the edge of his mind, Sean saw and rejected another scenario. Harry could just be a decent man, clumsily trying to be friendly and not knowing how because he was being pushed to the limits by Sean. As for Tom, he could be torn both ways, part of him wanting to despise Sean and part of him wanting to like him. But Sean didn't really want to see this more rational explanation, preferring the high drama of conspiracy, the black and white of good and evil, and the optimistic thought that if only he could get rid of Harry and Tom then Dad might find a reason to return. But first of all the enemy had to be defeated.

By the time Sean arrived at the park, there seemed to be a suffocating lack of air amongst the well-ordered, close-cut lawns and regimented beds with their ranks of orderly flowers. A concrete path ran around the perimeter, signposted to the Wild

Wood which, as Sean knew, wasn't wild at all, only containing a few stunted trees and some dusty-looking foliage.

He had arranged to meet Tom by the bandstand which hadn't seen a concert in years and was now filled with empty cans, sweet wrappers and what appeared to be part of a washing machine.

He glanced at his watch – he was ten minutes late, but surely Tom wouldn't have given up and gone home already?

Sean stood by the bandstand, waiting for Tom to show up, but after a few minutes, he began to wonder if Tom could be winding him up again, playing some kind of feeble joke.

He was about to give up and go home when he heard a whistle, soft but persistent. He gazed around him. It sounded as if it was coming from the scrubby foliage in the Wild Wood.

'Is that you, Tom?'

There was silence, except for the rustling of leaves in the dry breeze.

'Tom? Why don't you stop messing about? I didn't come up here to play games.' He was very tense now, sure that something was going to happen. But what? He didn't trust Tom, especially after the events of the past few days, and now he was unsure what to do.

Reluctantly, Sean began to walk towards the scrub, breaking into a run as he neared the wood. Glancing back he saw a man walking his dog, but there was no one else around.

Not looking where he was going, Sean almost tripped over the rusting frame of an old bike that had been abandoned beside the path. The Wild Wood had become a local tip. There was a rancid smell of wild garlic, and Sean scratched his hand on an enormous thistle. The scruffy, dusty little wood seemed to crowd in on him. Suddenly he smelt something that overlaid the wild garlic, but although it was familiar he couldn't think what it was. Panic swept over him and he felt an inexplicable desire to run. But he had to find Tom first. As Sean's agitation increased it slowly dawned on him what the smell was. Had he been trying to ignore it, to banish the burning from his mind?

He came to a stumbling halt, seeing flames burst from the upholstery of a sofa that had been dumped about fifty metres away. A dense cloud of black smoke drifted down the path towards him on the breeze. He choked and ran on, his heart pounding, his mouth dry.

Sean sprinted down a narrow path and entered a small thicket, but the way was barred by a fallen tree. Sean watched as snakes of bright orange flame, caught the dry bark.

At the top of the path, thick black smoke spiralled from the sofa, and in front of Sean the fallen tree crackled and burnt viciously, blocking his way, making his eyes stream. He whimpered, a sob in his throat. How had two separate fires started at once?

He would have to brave the nettles on the other side of the wood, it was the only way to get back to the safety of the open space. Sean was terrified. Then he saw a shadow running through the smoke, carrying something.

'Tom?' he shouted. 'Is that you, Tom?'

Why hadn't he seen the figure before? Had someone been hiding?

Sean paused, scanning the woods for the figure, but there was no one there. He knew hesitation was dangerous – the blaze was spreading, tongues of fire leaping through the tinder-dry foliage, and soon the wood could become an inferno, roasting him to a crisp.

*

Sean had a last look around and then plunged to the right, cutting through the nettles, feeling them stinging his hands. Several times he had to jump over abandoned junk, but soon he found himself running alongside the road, a high and impenetrable iron fence separating him from safety.

Sean increased his speed, finding a narrow path that led out of the wood to the broad expanse of grass. Once there, he continued to run until he was in the centre of the park where he stood choking and gasping.

The whole of the wood was alight now, flames shooting up the trees, branches snapping like gunshots and the roar of the fire becoming louder. Black smoke billowed over the road, bringing the traffic to a halt, and a chorus of horns merged with the crackling.

Then Sean saw Tom pounding across the park, panting and stiff-legged. Despite his football training, he seemed completely exhausted.

'Where have you been?' yelled Sean.

For a moment Tom couldn't reply as he struggled for breath. 'I've – called – the – fire – brigade –'

'Where were you? You weren't at the bandstand.'

'I was practising.'

'Practising what?'

'Running.'

'Where?'

'Round the park.'

'I didn't see you.'

The blazing wood was roaring noisily and Sean could see a crowd of curious spectators streaming through the park gates to get a closer look.

'I took a breather round the back of the cricket screen,' Tom spluttered.

'For how long?'

'I don't know. I lay down. I was knackered. Maybe ten minutes.'

'What did you do then?'

'You weren't around and I saw the wood was on fire, so I legged it to the phone box and dialled 999. Someone set fire to the wood.'

'It wasn't me.'

'Who said it was?' Tom gazed at Sean in amazement, his eyes narrowing.

Did he really suspect him, Sean wondered. He thought of all the fires that had started over the last few days – his singed duvet, the grass under the lab window, the fire in the kitchen, the toaster, the red-hot TV remote control. Then there were the distortions, the synchronised car lights and the TV set. And most of these happenings had been accompanied by the smell of burning. Now the whole wood was ablaze and he was right there when it happened. But none of them had anything to do with him. They couldn't have. They were all coincidences.

Startled rooks flew above the flames, making dismal cawing sounds, watching their nests being destroyed as a tree toppled to the ground. Then Sean and Tom both heard distant sirens.

'How did the fire start?' demanded Sean. 'I almost got trapped.'

'Why were you in there?' Tom sounded uneasy.

'I heard you whistle.'

'I wasn't anywhere near that wood.'

'You must have been.'

'I wasn't.'

They stared at each other with rising hostility as Sean wondered if Tom was playing some kind of game. Then they turned to watch the blaze as more people joined the crowd and the sirens came nearer. The smoke smelt toxic and Sean heard someone in the crowd say, 'There's more rubbish in that wood than trees. The council should have cleared the stuff months ago.'

Tom was gazing at the gates of the park and Sean

glanced at him curiously for he looked as if he was trying to make up his mind about something.

'You know what's going to happen, don't you?' he said suddenly and fearfully. 'We're going to get nicked.'

'Why?' asked Sean blankly.

'If we hang around here much longer it'll look as if we started the fire.'

Sean knew Tom was right and he could see the newspaper headline in the chaos of his mind: TEENAGERS START BLAZE.

'Let's go.'

'Don't start running,' Tom warned him. 'It'll make us look guilty. Stroll away casually, nice and easy. Follow me.'

Tom started to move away as if he was walking on burning coals, almost tip-toeing, swinging his arms in a peculiar way. No one could have looked more awkward, or guilty.

'Hang on, you two,' said a skinhead from the crowd. 'Where do you think you're going?'

'I've got to get back home,' said Sean, as Tom burst into a run.

'You're not going anywhere.' The skinhead grabbed Sean and twisted his arm up into a painful half-nelson, yelling to his mate, 'Get the other kid. I reckon they set fire to that wood.'

'So you torched the wood then? Which one of you did it? Or was it both of you?'

Sean didn't have an answer.

The crowd had been pushed back by police officers and Tom had been taken away and questioned by an officer who had introduced himself as PC Benson. Meanwhile Sean stood apprehensively beside PC Warren who was talking urgently into his personal radio. Sean didn't like what he heard.

'The fire's under control and we've got two suspects in their early teens. We're talking to them now. Over.'

The crowd had re-formed at the park gates where a couple of fire engines were parked, their long hoses snaking over the ground towards the wood. As they arched great jets of water into the blackened trees and foliage, steam rose menacingly, but there was only the odd tongue of flame remaining.

'What were you two lads doing here?' asked PC Warren. Sean began his own explanation, hoping it would match up with Tom's. He now understood why they were being kept apart, to check that they were telling the same story.

'We came up here to do some training,' he began.

'What kind of training?' asked PC Warren sceptically.

'Running. Tom asked me to train him.'

'So you know each other.'

'We're stepbrothers.'

'How come you're training him?'

'I'm a cross-country runner,' said Sean, trying to assert himself. 'I've won cups. Tom hasn't run before.'

'So you came to the park together?'

'Separately.'

'Why was that?'

'We don't live together.'

'Who arrived first?'

'I did,' said Sean and then realised he was contradicting what Tom had told him. 'What I mean is, he arrived first.'

'Make up your mind,' said PC Warren brusquely.

'Tom arrived first but I didn't see him.'

'Was he in the wood?'

'No. He was behind the cricket screen. That's why I couldn't see him.'

'Why was he hiding behind the cricket screen?'

'He wasn't hiding. He was taking a breather. He'd been running.'

'I thought you were going to teach him.'

'He was having a practice.'

'How long was he having this breather?'

'Ten minutes.'

'That's a long time. Hardly worth coaching him if he was so tired.'

'He had a stitch.'

There was a long pause during which Sean gazed down at the grass.

'So why did you go into the wood?' PC Warren's tone sharpened.

'Because I thought Tom was in there.'

'Playing a game with you?'

'I thought he was having a joke.'

'But you said he was behind the cricket screen.'

'He was, but I didn't know that then.' Sean's voice shook. 'I thought he might be in the wood.'

'Why?'

'I heard this whistle.'

'So what could Tom be doing in the wood?'

'Hiding,' said Sean shakily.

'From you?'

'Yes.'

'That's a funny sort of game for boys of your age.' PC Warren paused. 'So you found him in the wood?'

'No!' yelled Sean. 'I told you. Tom was behind the cricket screen.'

'So why did you go in the wood?'

'Because I thought he was hiding there. I told you that.'

There was a pause.

'OK. So when did you start the fire?' PC Warren asked abruptly.

'I didn't.' Sean trembled. The futility of the situation was obvious. What was Mum going to say?

'Enjoyed watching the wood burn, did you?'

'No!'

'Bit of fun that got out of hand?'

'I didn't do it,' yelled Sean, suddenly even more afraid than he had been before. PC Warren seemed to be twisting his words, trying to trap him. 'I didn't set fire to the wood!'

'You *were* in the wood, weren't you, lad? You've got a dirty face. Looks like wood smoke to me.'

'I *told* you I was in there. Looking for Tom and then the fire started.'

'Just like that?' asked PC Warren.

'What do you mean?'

'The fire started on its own?'

'No. Yes.'

'Give me a straight answer.'

'It *seemed* to start on its own.'

'You mean *you* started it?'

'No. I haven't got any matches.' Sean was panicking now, the sweat streaming down his face. 'You can search me.' Glancing at Tom, he had a horrible feeling that their stories were not matching up in any way.

'Maybe you rubbed two sticks together, like a boy scout.'

'I didn't start the fire.'

There was a long silence which was finally broken by PC Warren. 'You've done a lot of damage, haven't you, Sean? That was a lovely little wood.'

'I didn't –'

'So I think you and your mate –'

'Stepbrother.'

'You and your stepbrother should come down to the station so we can ask you a few more questions and get you to sign a statement.'

'What about my mother?'

'You can phone her at the station.'

'Will we be kept in over night?' asked Sean miserably, thinking of a bare cell, bread and water and a lice-infested bed.

'You won't if you tell us the truth.' PC Warren seemed to seize on his anxiety, adding it to his arsenal of weapons.

'I've *told* you the truth.'

'Come on then,' said PC Warren. 'We can all have a nice cup of tea down at the station.' He took Sean by the arm, and as they walked towards one of the police cars he noticed Tom was being taken to another. They exchanged glances.

The crowd watched their progress with growing hostility until someone shouted out, 'Vandals!' The cry was taken up and a threatening chant began. As the car edged its way through the spectators, Sean noticed that their eyes were full of a combination of pleasure and outrage.

Sean knew that the excitement was a break in routine and that he and Tom had brought drama into the crowd's dull lives. But why had Tom really asked him down to the park? Could it have been part of an overall plan he had hatched with Harry? Had Tom started the fire and then made it look as if he had done it? The enemy was winning hands down.

Sean tried to reason with himself. Why would they have gone to such lengths? Of course they hadn't. It was all too ridiculous for words. That was another well-worn phrase of Mum's. Too ridiculous for words. But was it?

'Quite a lynch mob,' commented PC Warren as the spectators fell back to let the cars pass.

'I didn't do it,' muttered Sean. 'I didn't start the fire.'

'We'll sort that out down at the station.'

What was Mum going to think, he wondered. So far this week he'd been suspended from school for fighting, thrown brown sauce at his stepfather, and now he was being accused of setting fire to a wood. It was ridiculous. He hadn't set fire to anything in his life.

As the police car drove out of the park, PC Warren asked, 'Got anything to tell me, son?' Had he noticed how hard Sean was thinking?

Sean shook his head.

10

Things are getting weirder and weirder. I've just practically been arrested for burning down a wood! I can say this categorically. I never started the fire. I'm terrified of fires and I don't understand why they keep happening. It could have been Tom, though. He was probably trying to set me up.

The police station was modern and spacious with banks of computers and almost as many potted plants. Sean already felt like a criminal and he couldn't bear to think how his mother was going to react to all this. Glancing back he saw Tom, and Sean told himself he must have been crazy to think for one moment that he had set him up. After all, he was being brought in for questioning too and what was Harry going to say about that?

Sean was taken to a small and grubby-looking interview room with only a calendar on the off-white wall and chairs placed each side of a desk.

PC Warren came in with him and sat down. He pulled a phone from the drawer and plugged it into the wall socket saying, 'I can't start interviewing you until your parents arrive. Would you like to ring them?' He was coldly official and there was no expression on his face at all.

'Have I been arrested?' asked Sean.

'Not yet.'

A glimmer of hope penetrated his troubled and confused mind. 'I'd like to ring my dad.'

'What about your mother?'

'They're divorced.'

'Where does your dad live?'

'In Southampton.'

'And your mum?'

'Just down the road.'

'Ring her then.'

'I don't want to,' insisted Sean. 'I want to ring my dad.' He was determined now, and PC Warren frowned impatiently.

'It's too far for him to come.'

'I want to ring him!' persisted Sean. But rather than feeling anger, he felt as if he was going to cry.

'Ring your mum now and speak to your dad later.' There was some warmth in PC Warren's voice at last.

'Can I speak to Mum in private?'

'Sorry.'

Grimly, Sean gave in and dialled home. 'Mum?'

'You've been gone a long time. Still with Tom, are you?'

'Sort of. I –'

'By the way, the repair man came round and said the TV set was faulty, and there was something wrong with the remote control. He didn't have time to look at the toaster. He's taken the TV away and left us another. When are you coming back?'

'Mum –'

'What is it?' Now she was sensing trouble.

'There's this wood.'

'What wood?'

'In the park.'

'Well?'

'The police think I set it on fire.'

'*What?*'

'But I didn't.'

'Where are you now?' Mum sounded efficient and decisive and not in the least critical. Sean was surprised.

'At the police station.'

'Where's Tom?'

'He's here too.'

There was a short silence and then she said briskly, without a trace of panic or emotion,

'I'm coming straight down.'

'Hang on,' said PC Warren. 'I'd like a word. Mrs Chambers? Your son has to sign a statement and, by law, you need to be here. Do you want me to send a car? I do understand your concern, and, no, he hasn't been charged. His stepbrother is down here too, but my colleague will be in touch about him. I gather his father is your husband. Yes. I'll see you in a little while.' He looked up at Sean. 'We'll have to wait,' said PC Warren. 'Now, how about that nice cup of tea?'

'Can't I see Tom?'

'I'm afraid we still have to keep you two apart. That's the only way we're going to get the truth, isn't it?'

Sean spent the next half hour sitting in the interview room on his own, staring down at a scummy looking cup of tea that had a horrible treacly taste. He was now so exhausted that his mind seemed to have blanked out, just like it had on the flight home from a trip he and Mum and Dad had taken to Disneyland in California. The journey had been so long that Sean had become glazed and numb, as if he was only half alive and couldn't react to anything or anyone.

Ten minutes passed and he kept looking at his watch, imagining Tom sitting in another, identical interview room, doing much the same.

Dully, Sean was sure he had contradicted himself so many times that he wouldn't be able to remember what he had said. Tom had probably made a mess of it too.

Twenty minutes later, Mum arrived, escorted by PC Warren who had a long-suffering look. 'It's outrageous,' she was saying. 'How dare you treat my son like this? Dragging him back here –'

'I didn't drag him anywhere, madam. You can understand that with the two boys in close proximity to the fire we had no other choice but to –'

'Aren't you even going to have the common decency to tell Sean what's happened?'

PC Warren put a heavy hand on Sean's shoulder. 'It's all right, son. You're free to go. Someone else has confessed to starting the fire –'

'Who?' Could the confession have been made by Tom?

'A vagrant's got this thing against the local authority. He's been going round burning down their property. Cricket pavilion, public toilets, and now he's confessed to burning the Wild Wood.'

'I didn't see anyone around,' said Sean. Then he remembered the shadowy figure in the smoke and suddenly realised he had forgotten all about him. 'I just remembered,' he said. 'I did see someone running through the wood.'

'Why didn't you tell me?' demanded PC Warren.

'I forgot, but you wouldn't have believed me anyway.'

He shrugged. 'That guy's pretty nippy on his feet, I gather. Anyway, he's given himself up.'

But Mum had no intention of leaving it at that. 'My son would never behave like a vandal, and neither would Tom. I'm going to make an official complaint.'

'You have every right to do that, madam. But I must advise you that PC Benson and I were only doing our duty. Property has to be protected and –'

'My son needs protection too,' said Mum sharply. 'From people like you.'

Sean began to worry that his mother was going to lose her temper and get them both into more trouble.

'I'm sorry you see it that way, madam.' PC Warren was trying to be tolerant.

'I'll shall be writing to the Chief Constable.

You've no right to go round arresting innocent children.'

'Juveniles are causing a great deal of damage in this area,' said PC Warren.

'Not my son!'

'Please, be sensible and take him home.' PC Warren put a hand on her arm and with a visible effort she fought for control and regained her temper. But as she did so, Sean could smell burning and saw a wisp of smoke curling from the wastepaper basket. Glancing at his mother, he saw that she was staring down at the wastepaper basket too. Then the smoke became a flame. A familiar icy hand seemed to clutch at Sean's stomach. Fire and ice, he thought. Fire and ice.

PC Warren gazed at the blaze in amazement and then quickly strode over to the basket, tipped the contents out on to the scarred linoleum and stamped on the flames until they were extinguished, sending bits of burnt paper fluttering around the interview room.

'Someone must have chucked a smouldering fag in there,' he announced, turning to Sean with a sour smile. 'Were you smoking?'

'Of course I wasn't,' he replied indignantly. 'I

don't smoke. You can search me if you like.'

'Then how did this lot burst into flame?'

'Someone must have been smoking in here before,' snapped Mum, ready to resume battle.

PC Warren went to the door and shouted down the corridor, 'PC Clayton?'

A young policewoman emerged from one of the interview rooms.

'Were you interviewing George Spriggs in here?'

'Yes.'

'Smoking, was he?'

'I let him have a couple while I took his statement. What's the problem?'

'He must have chucked a fag into the wastepaper basket. Smouldered away and just burst into flame.'

'Blimey!'

'Lucky I was resourceful and stamped it out.'

'You deserve a medal.'

'Maybe you'd like to nominate me.' PC Warren closed the door, giving them both a warm smile. 'Looks as if I'm going to have to apologise again, doesn't it, Sean? So, you're *not* a pyrokinetic.'

'What are you accusing him of now?' said Mum suspiciously.

'What *is* a pyrokinetic?' asked Sean curiously.

'I'm only joking,' said PC Warren hastily. 'I just enjoy reading about the paranormal. It's a little hobby of mine. Apparently pyrokinetics can start fires by using their mental energy.' He looked doubtfully at Mrs Chambers, realising his joke wasn't going down very well.

'That's a load of rubbish,' said Mum.

'Of course it is.' He shrugged.

Mum raised her eyebrows. 'Fancy joking at a time like this,' she said impatiently. 'It just emphasises how irresponsible you are. I'll be sending you a copy of our letter to the Chief Constable.'

They met up with a disgruntled Harry and Tom on the way out of the police station.

'It was all a mistake,' said Tom, looking relieved. 'Some vagrant started the fire.'

'It's disgraceful,' muttered Harry as they walked towards the car. 'We'll both make a formal complaint.'

Mum agreed. 'They're not getting away with it. Our boys were arrested in public. Any of our friends could have seen what happened and they'll assume the worst.'

Our boys. The phrase made Sean instantly angry,

but then a new uneasiness gripped him. All these coincidences were so unsettling. Suppose Mum and Harry thought he *had* started the fires, to get back at Harry, and they were both covering up their suspicions?

'You *know* I didn't start that fire, Mum, don't you?'

'Of course you didn't.' But wasn't there a hint of defence in her voice? Wasn't she being too emphatic?

'What about Harry?' demanded Sean.

'The police say you didn't do it. The police say Tom didn't do it. They've got someone else. What are you worrying about?'

But wasn't Harry being too restrained? Wasn't he holding back his real suspicions?

Sean had to talk to someone. But who? Would Tom know if Harry suspected Sean was running a campaign against him?

Directly they got home, Mum and Harry began to compose a letter of complaint to the Chief Constable, while Tom and Sean sat in uneasy alliance, eating sandwiches.

'Why don't you come up to my room and have a talk before you go?' Sean asked tentatively.

'Not for long.' But Tom followed him upstairs willingly enough and slumped on the bed with his shoes on.

'We've had all these fires.'

'I know that.' Tom stared up at him, his expression hard to read.

'Does your dad think I started them?'

'Why should he?'

'To scare him away.'

Tom looked uneasy, shrugging his shoulders and staring down at the floor. 'You'd have to be mad to do that. Like burn down your own home.'

'Suppose your dad thinks I hate him? That I'd do anything to get rid of him?'

'I told you, only a nutter would do that.'

'All those weird things that happened.' Sean paused, already sensing that Tom was dismissing him as some kind of crackpot. But it seemed too late to stop. 'There must be an explanation. I didn't start the fires even if your dad thinks I did.'

'Who says he thinks you did?'

'I do.' Sean knew he was plunging in too deep.

Tom got to his feet. 'I think you're a right idiot and I'm going home. Why can't you get it into your head that no one, including my dad, thinks you started those fires?'

'Thanks for listening.' Sean was sarcastic, but Tom pushed past him, hurrying towards the door.

'You're turning into a real weirdo.'

'Thanks again.'

Tom thudded down the stairs and Sean tried to wipe off all the dirty marks Tom had made with his shoes on the bed, desperately wishing he hadn't tried to confide in him, grimly aware that tomorrow everyone at school would know what a fool he was. Tom had been given a weapon and Sean was sure he would use it.

He put a CD on and then took it off again, trying to settle down to some homework and failing as he heard the sound of voices downstairs and then the front door closing. Had Tom been telling Mum and Harry what a weirdo he was?

A few minutes later, his mother came up, looking slightly flustered. 'Are you all right, love?'

'What's Tom told you?'

'Nothing.'

'He told you I was a weirdo. Didn't he?'

'You're just upset,' she said placatingly. 'You've both had a terrible experience. But Harry and I are writing to the Chief Constable. That'll sort things out.'

Sean knew it wouldn't sort anything out, but he

didn't want to say any more as his mother was gazing at him anxiously.

'I hope this isn't going to put up another barrier between you and Tom.'

'Of course it won't. We're good mates now,' he lied. 'But, Mum, you've got to tell me. Does Harry think I started those fires? Do you?'

'Listen to me, Sean.' Mum was firm. 'Stop talking rubbish. You're exhausted. Now get some sleep.'

That night, Sean dreamt he was watching the burning crops again, but instead of the blazing suburbs of London on the horizon, there was an ocean of flames, the waves cresting fire.

He woke hot and sweating, and with a sickening jolt saw the duvet was singed again. He hadn't lit the candle last night as he'd been too tired to read, so how could this have happened? Soon Mum was bound to find out about his duvet and what would she do? Years ago, when he was much younger, Sean had gone though a spell of wetting the bed and then she had been very sympathetic. But wasn't this rather different? Sean studied the mark closely. Perhaps he'd got it wrong and the duvet was no more singed than before, although the mark certainly looked as if it had grown bigger.

Exhausted by his confused thoughts and doubts, Sean opened the curtains to find the sun was high in the sky, and in the clear light of day his anxieties lessened. What *had* he been going on about last night? Dropping himself in it like that. What a load of rubbish. No wonder Tom thought he was a weirdo.

11

Wednesday, 7th

I feel better this morning. I've been a real fool. I know I didn't start any fires. I'm scared of fire. But what worries me is confiding in Tom. Now he thinks I'm a real weirdo. Will he tell everyone at school?

Harry was at the breakfast table, the letter to the Chief Constable spread out in front of him, obviously wanting to read the contents aloud, but Sean, who now had a blazing headache, didn't want to know.

'Well,' said Mum as she came in with a new pot of tea. 'Who's been burning the midnight oil then?'

Harry smiled hopefully. 'Would you like to hear what we've written?'

'I haven't got time,' Sean snapped.

'Of course you have. You don't normally leave until ten to.'

'I've got to get in early today. There's a cross-country meeting.'

'It won't take a sec,' pleaded Mum. 'Harry's been

up half the night writing the letter. He wants to support you.'

'I haven't got time to listen to it now. Read it to me when I get home.'

Mum sighed and Harry looked hurt. 'I've done a lot of work on your behalf, Sean.'

Sean grabbed his blazer, shrugged it on and picked up his bag. 'I've got to go.'

'Sit down and listen. I want to post the letter today, strike while the iron's hot.'

'See you later.'

'I suppose you're full of those crazy ideas Tom was telling us about last night,' said Harry, irritated by Sean's lack of interest.

So Tom *had* gone straight downstairs last night and told them everything. He could imagine the scene, with Harry and Tom laughing together and Mum looking embarrassed. The anger seared across his mind. 'I'll get him for that.'

'I don't want any more trouble,' said his mother, blinking back the tears. 'Tom's worried about you, that's all.'

'Why?' asked Sean in a steely voice, determined to find out what had happened.

'He was just concerned you were under a lot of stress,' interrupted Harry. 'I'm sorry about what I said just now. Please, don't play the giddy goat, just listen to the letter I've –'

'The what?' Sean gave a snort of derisive laughter.

'The giddy goat,' repeated Harry, flushing slightly as Mum laughed too.

'I've never heard that expression before,' she giggled.

'Well, you've heard it now.' Harry suddenly thumped the table with his fist and the sauce bottle fell over, but luckily the cap was firmly in place this time.

'Watch it!' said Sean, still laughing. 'We don't want another accident.'

'Last time wasn't an accident,' bellowed Harry. 'You ruined my best shirt.'

'I've got to go, Mum.' Sean turned to the door.

'Come back.' Harry stood up.

'I can't be late.'

'Come back here!' He made a futile grab for Sean's shoulder.

'Let go of me!' His temper flashed again, hard and bright like burnished steel.

'I've been up half the night with this letter!'

'Push off.'

'How dare you speak to me like that.' Harry

gripped Sean's shoulder and swung him round.

'Let him go,' yelled Mum. 'You're making him angry.'

Angry, thought Sean. You don't know what anger is. Or at least Harry doesn't, and now he's going to find out.

He pushed his stepfather away as hard as he could and Harry staggered into the breakfast table with a crash of breaking china. Sean ran from the room and hurried out of the front door before he could see the full extent of the disaster.

12

Sean ran through the estate as fast as he could, his head pounding, the streets bent and distorted and etched in crimson red. Houses, shops, traffic and pedestrians began to melt in front of his eyes, until everything and everyone had merged into a sticky mass. Then there was a snapping sound in his mind, like an over-stretched elastic band, and his surroundings returned to normal, leaving a strong smell of burning.

Sean gazed round apprehensively, and saw with a tremendous shock and then a rush of panic that a tiny Fiat had pulled into the curb with a screech of brakes, smoke billowing from the engine. Inside, a young woman was at the wheel, her mouth open in a silent scream, her baby strapped into a seat in the back. The smoke increased and suddenly Sean could see a finger of bright red flame.

Although the street was crowded, only a few people turned to give the car a curious glance. Why didn't the mother get out, wondered Sean. The car could explode at any moment and she and the baby would be killed. Then he realised that she must be too terrified to move and that someone had to get to her fast. He glanced at the passers-by, most of whom were just bustling on, and for a moment he hesitated.

Then a huge flame burst from the Fiat's engine and Sean rushed towards the driver's door. The young mother was beating at the window now, her terrified eyes fixed on his while Sean wrenched at the door which wouldn't open. Then he realised the automatic lock was on and desperately wondered what kind of security she had. There was a central locking device on the dashboard in his father's car. Sean began to pound at the window, pointing at where he thought the switch might be, but the woman was too terrified by the flames and the smoke and the screams of her baby to pay him any attention.

He thumped at the window, refusing to give up. 'You've locked the doors! Push the switch on the dashboard.'

The woman turned to stare at him numbly, not taking in what he was saying.

'You've locked the doors,' Sean yelled again, noticing the baby was going blue in the face. 'Push the switch on the dashboard.'

She pulled herself together, shook off at least a little of her panic and wound down the driver's window. By this time a small crowd had gathered and were watching passively, with morbid interest. For a moment Sean turned and gazed into their detached blank faces. Could they really be human? Maybe they were ghouls from outer space, disguised in human clothing, drawn to disaster, needing to stare and never, ever help.

Sean shouted his instructions again and this time the young mother nodded frantically. She pulled a switch on the dashboard and the locks snapped up.

The crowd fell back as more flames shot from the engine while Sean wrenched open the rear door and fumbled at the screaming baby's harness without success. He had no idea how to undo it but he was quickly pushed aside by the young woman. She pressed a catch and dragged her baby to safety, standing trembling on the pavement with the child howling in her arms.

'Thank you,' she gasped. 'You wonderful, wonderful boy.'

She planted a kiss on Sean's cheek and he went bright scarlet in the face. As the flames consumed the Fiat he heard the sound of sirens and a fire engine and a patrol car drew up. So someone *had* called the rescue services after all.

'Get back!' came the cry, and realising the danger at last the crowd scattered self-protectively.

A familiar figure stepped out of the patrol car and PC Warren gazed in astonishment at the sight of Sam and the burning car.

'I just don't believe this,' he said as the fire brigade began to hose down the burning Fiat. 'You again! Where's your stepbrother?'

'He's not here.'

'But you are.'

'He's been very brave,' said the young mother. 'I was totally spaced out and forgot to release the central locking. Liam and I could have been burnt to death if it hadn't been for this boy. He deserves a medal.'

With considerable satisfaction, Sean watched the expression on PC Warren's face change.

'If we all move away,' he said woodenly, 'I'd better take some notes.'

The young woman shakily introduced herself as Sarah Henshaw and began to tell PC Warren exactly what had happened.

Eventually he snapped his notebook shut and turned to Sean, who was watching the fire brigade pumping foam over the Fiat as more police officers arrived to hold off the ghoulish crowd. 'You've turned out to be a right little hero, haven't you?'

'I'll be in trouble for being late,' said Sean anxiously.

'If you give me the number I'll phone the school and tell them what's happened,' said PC Warren as Mrs Henshaw hugged her baby close.

Meanwhile, a fire officer was examining the still smoking engine.

'What happened?' Mrs Henshaw asked. 'Why did my car burst into flames like that?'

'I can't say for sure, but these leads are burnt right through. It's possible there might have been an electrical fault.'

As Mrs Henshaw planted another kiss on Sean's cheek, PC Warren looked strangely at Sean and said exactly what he'd been thinking himself.

'Funny thing, coincidence, isn't it?'

13

A special afternoon assembly had been called and most students were apprehensive. Sean, still unnerved by what had happened, hardly able to believe he had been involved in yet another fire, had been inattentive in class all morning, incurring the wrath of his teacher but not really caring. The duvet, the grass, the kitchen, the wood and now the car. All burning bright. How did that poem go?

Tiger, tiger, burning bright,
In the forest of the night -

Where was it all going to end?

'There's going to be trouble,' said one of the prefects with relish as they filed down the corridor to the hall. 'Someone's for the high jump for sure.'

Sean was trying to keep out of Tom's way, but to his irritation he saw he was just ahead of him. As if by instinct, Tom turned, slowed down and waited for Sean and they walked down the corridor together. He seemed superficially friendly, but Sean could detect an angry impatience in Tom that was just under the surface; he kept darting glances at Sean, as if he was about to say something and was wondering if he should.

Sean hadn't told anyone at school about the car fire – it was all too weird. Besides, the thought of the row at home and the fact that he would have to return there soon and probably have another argument, depressed him just as much as his other grisly thoughts.

Sean wondered if Tom knew about the argument over the letter, and wasn't left in doubt for long. 'You should leave my dad alone,' he suddenly announced aggressively.

Sean sighed. He could hardly pretend that he hadn't touched his stepfather, but at least he could try to explain why he'd done it. He wondered if Harry had been up to the school. Had he seen Mr Jenkins? Had the special assembly been called as a result? Was he going to be put on display?

Sean decided to plead ignorance. 'I don't know what you're talking about.'

'I went to see him at work at lunchtime.'

'What for?'

'I don't see as much of him as I used to. Remember?'

What about my father, thought Sean bitterly. I only see him once a fortnight. Why was Tom always so selfish? But this time he didn't feel anger, only loneliness and isolation.

All Sean wanted to do was go home, get into bed and pull the duvet over his head. But then he might dream about fire and wake to find his duvet singed and then the coincidences would start up all over again. Sean reckoned his life was fast becoming a circular trap from which there seemed no way out.

'So why did you push my dad like that?' demanded Tom.

'He provoked me.'

'How?'

'Going on about that letter to the Chief Constable.'

'He was only trying to help.' Tom was indignant.

'Your father was going to make me late and then he grabbed me. If he ever does that again he'll get the same.' Sean couldn't bring himself to mention Harry by name.

'Can't you try to get on with him?' asked Tom, suddenly sounding more reasonable.

Sean felt guilty. 'It'll be OK if he doesn't touch me. Why don't you tell him?'

'He really is trying.'

'Trying what?' Sean muttered.

'To get on with you. Why don't you *ever* think

about anyone else? I've lost Dad to you lot, you know that, don't you?'

'*What?*' Sean was shocked to see the expression of misery in Tom's eyes.

'I've lost him to you,' he repeated.

'You haven't,' Sean protested. He was suddenly aware of how selfish he'd been. Had he ever seen the situation from Tom's point of view? Of course he hadn't. He'd been too engulfed with jealousy and anger.

'No?' Tom glanced at him cynically.

'You can see him any time you like.'

'But he's not living with us, is he? He's living with you. That's what counts.'

'I think you're forgetting something.' Sean's anger sparked and he lost any desire to understand Tom's sufferings. 'I can only see my dad once a fortnight and I have to go all the way down to Southampton. Just think about that.'

'You can still ring him.' Tom became truculent as they walked into the crowded hall.

'Big deal.'

'Besides –'

'Besides what?'

'It's his fault he's in Southampton, isn't it?' Tom spoke slowly and maliciously. 'He was seeing someone down there, wasn't he? Probably still is. My dad didn't do anything like that. He and Mum just couldn't –' But he didn't finish his sentence for Sean's hands were locked tight around his throat.

Tom's eyes dilated as he tried to kick out at Sean's ankles. Some students had already noticed what was going on and were turning round in their seats, hardly able to believe another fight was about to begin.

'Now what's going on here?' a teacher demanded as he strode towards them. Sean reluctantly released Tom who clutched at his throat, gasping for air.

'Only mucking about, sir.'

The teacher, who didn't know either of them, had been instructed to get everyone sitting down as soon as possible and couldn't be bothered to look into the matter any further.

'Well, go and sit down,' he snarled. 'Mr Jenkins wants to make a start.'

Mr Jenkins stood on the stage, gazing down at his curious students, looking composed yet severe. Sean wondered yet again if his assault on his stepfather was going to be made public. Surely Mr

Jenkins wouldn't discuss his private life at assembly. Or would he?

'Boys and girls, it's not often that I have the opportunity to report something dramatic to you. But I'm delighted to say that a heroic act of bravery was carried out by one of our students.' Mr Jenkins paused as a buzz of excitement and interest began to fill the hall. 'This morning, a mother and baby were trapped inside a blazing vehicle in the high street. With startling initiative, one of our students helped them both to safety.'

Sean felt complete surprise, as if Mr Jenkins was talking about someone else. He then felt a rush of embarrassment.

Mr Jenkins paused for effect and then held up a hand for silence as Sean gazed up at him anxiously.

'Mrs Henshaw, the young mother in question, phoned me this morning, as did a police officer who attended the scene, and they both underlined the bravery of our pupil and asked me to praise him publicly.' He paused again. 'That boy is Sean Fields, and, Sean, I'd like you to join me on stage.'

Spontaneous applause broke out as Sean shakily stood up, almost tripped over someone's feet, and walked awkwardly towards the steps.

*

Mr Jenkins shook Sean's hand. 'Thank you, on behalf of the driver, Mrs Henshaw, and PC Warren. You're very much the hero and I called your mother at home to tell her so.'

Sean felt a surge of joy, but glancing down into the audience he saw Tom sitting there and all his pleasure and pride immediately evaporated. The raw loathing on his stepbrother's face was deeply threatening. Sean spent the rest of the afternoon being slapped on the back and applauded. Everyone, apart from Tom, wanted to shake his hand, but he couldn't blame Tom – after all, he'd nearly strangled him.

14

*I can hardly believe what happened. That
mother and baby could have been burnt
to death in their car. At least the burning
car couldn't have had anything to do with
me. Could it? Now I'm a hero. I couldn't
believe it when Jenkins called me up to
the front - I felt really proud. But Tom
hates me. I could see the hatred in his
eyes. Well, I did half-strangle him. Perhaps
I should make more of an effort to be
friends.*

Sean put the diary back under his bed and sat
down, a mass of confused thoughts churning away
in his head. Suddenly there was a knock on the
door and Mum and Harry appeared.

'One,' said Harry.

'Two.' Mum was smiling radiantly.

'Three,' they shouted together as Harry showed
Sean the local paper. The front page headline read:

WHO'S A HERO?
SEAN IS

'Well done, love,' said Mum, throwing her arms

round him, while Harry stood awkwardly behind her. Sean had to swallow hard so as not to let his voice break as he said, 'Thanks.' He thought he sounded rather feeble so he thanked them again.

'We're proud of you,' said Harry and Sean was sure now that he was completely sincere.

'I've made a special tea,' said Mum.

'Corned-beef fritters?'

'Are you tired of them? I can always do something else.'

Mum was getting agitated and he hurriedly reassured her. 'No. I love them.'

Harry got up and headed for the door. 'Come down as soon as you can.' Sean knew he would be boasting about him in the supermarket tomorrow. But did that really matter?

'Harry –'

'Yes?'

'I'm sorry about what happened this morning.'

'Think nothing of it.'

'But I *am* sorry.'

'Look, we both lost our tempers. The trouble is yours is a bit more sparky than mine, that's all.'

That's not a bad word for it, thought Sean. He used to have a slow fuse, but now he always seemed to be lashing out.

'Have a glass of wine,' suggested Harry as they sat round the table in the kitchen.

'No, thanks.'

'Oh, go on. Do you good.'

'I don't like the taste.'

'You might get to like it.'

'No way.'

'Fancy a beer?'

'I'll just have a glass of coke.'

'Rot your teeth.'

Sean tried to control his irritation, but it was no good. Why wouldn't Harry just leave him alone? Then he remembered half-strangling Tom and wondered if his stepfather knew about that. Maybe he'd better confess now.

'Well,' said Harry, raising his glass. 'Here's to the hero.'

'I didn't do much.'

'That mother and baby could have been burnt to death,' said Mum.

'She got herself out.'

'You know what I mean.' She smiled at him so warmly that Sean felt a surge of love for her, and he didn't even mind when she turned to Harry and squeezed his arm. 'Let's make this brave act of Sean's a fresh start then,' she said. 'For all three of us.'

Why did she have to say that? thought Sean, and he felt his anger returning. Surely he wasn't going to be stuck with Harry for the rest of his life? It was an unbearable idea. A *hideous* thought and he wouldn't put up with it, not for anyone, even Mum. Sean wanted his dad back, now, and the impossibility of it happening made him boil with rage.

'I'll drink to that.' Harry raised his glass and then paused. 'What's that burning smell?' he asked. 'Did you leave something on the cooker?' Mum got up and dashed over to the frying pan while Harry turned to Sean and said patronisingly, 'That's women for you.'

Panic seized him as Mum threw a wet towel over the frying pan and it sizzled and hissed, sending out clouds of dense smoke.

'I've got something to tell you,' said Sean, trying to pull himself together.

'What's that?'

'I lost my temper with Tom again and I'm sorry.'

'I expect he can take it,' replied Harry with amazing tolerance.

The smoke from the frying pan rose in a thick haze.

'Sorry about that,' Mum said, returning to the

table, flushed and slightly out of breath. 'It'll clear in a minute. Now what were we saying?'

'I was saying I lost my temper with Tom,' began Sean again.

'Look,' said Harry. 'Stop worrying. You two are going to have to sort it out with our help. We must have some outings together. All four of us.'

Sean nodded miserably, but felt calmer. All he wanted was for life to go back to normal, to a time of Mum and Dad and not Harry and Tom. But he knew that wasn't going to happen and he would have to make the best of what he'd got.

'And now,' said Harry. 'We've got a little surprise for you. Step this way.'

Mystified, Sean followed his mother and stepfather down the garden to the shed.

Harry opened the door, switched on the light, and to his amazement Sean saw a brand new mountain bike, one of the most expensive models with an amazing number of gears and shiny paintwork.

'It's yours, son.' Sean didn't wince until later, for he felt completely overwhelmed. He had never owned anything like this. All he had ever had was a beaten-up old racer which had practically fallen to bits and he hardly used it now.

'Harry got a discount at the supermarket,' said Mum.

'Lucky we had them in stock.' His stepfather was all smiles. 'Tom helped me choose the colour.'

The bike was painted red. Like a flame.

Despite his excitement, Sean felt a nagging doubt. Why had Harry got Tom to choose the colour? And why had he chosen red? But on the other hand what was wrong with red? Colours weren't significant.

Trying to act normally he flung his arms round his mother and then hastily shook hands with the beaming Harry who was looking hopeful, willing him to like the bike, and, more importantly, to like him too. He's trying to buy my love, thought Sean. On the other hand, the bike was just so cool.

'Has Tom got a bike too?' he asked, although he had never seen him riding one.

'He will have,' said Harry. 'He's going to have a similar model for his birthday next month.'

Was it right that he had got his first, wondered Sean. Wasn't Tom going to be jealous? But there was no time to ask. Harry was already insisting he rode round the garden in the dark, which he did self-consciously, genuinely worried about Tom. Did he know he was going to get a mountain bike for his birthday, every bit as splendid as his own? And if he didn't…

When they got back inside Harry once again offered Sean a glass of wine and he politely refused. He didn't *want* to be loosened up and taken off his guard. Not by his stepfather, anyway. He still didn't trust him, despite the bike.

Harry raised his glass. 'So here's to us.'

Sean squirmed.

15

Thursday, 8th. 6.00 AM

Last night I dreamt I was standing on the edge of a volcano, gazing down into a fiery furnace as sheets of flame belched out around me. But I was completely untouched, even by the sudden flow of lava that welled up from the interior and splashed and steamed around my feet.

Sean woke to the sound of screaming. As he lay rigidly under his duvet, he thought at first that the sound came from an animal. Could something have been attacked by a fox? A cat? A dog? A rabbit?

As the screams continued, Sean heard Harry, getting out of bed, cursing, accompanied by Mum who sounded calmer and more alert.

Then, to his horror, Sean heard another noise, a crackling noise. Fire!

Sean was first out of the house, running down the garden to the shed where snakes of flame were devouring the whole structure hungrily. Something was crawling about on the lawn, making a low moaning sound – just like a wounded animal. But the something was human.

Then Sean realised with a chill of horror he was gazing down at Tom, and that his stepbrother was in the most appalling pain.

'I got burnt.' Tom rolled over on his back and held up a pair of blackened hands from which Sean recoiled. They were horrible. Like charcoal sticks.

'What happened?'

'You've got to help me,' Tom groaned piteously, writhing about on the grass.

'I'll call an ambulance.' Sean ran back to the house, cannoning into Harry who had a fire extinguisher in his hand.

'Who's out there?' he was yelling, as Mum joined him. 'Some vandal?'

'It's Tom. He's burnt his hands. I'm going to call an ambulance.'

Harry gave a little whimper of anguish, running over to his son and kneeling down beside him. Mum grabbed the fire extinguisher and kicked open the door of the shed, staggering back from the intense heat but steadily unleashing the foam.

*

As they waited for the ambulance to arrive, Tom sobbed with pain in his father's arms. Although his mother had managed to put out the fire, all that was left of Sean's precious new mountain bike was a charred frame and wheels.

Harry looked up at Sean.

'Tom was jealous of the bike,' he muttered. 'He lit a bottle of kerosene, broke the window and struck a match. He didn't realise it would ignite so quickly. Just look at those hands.'

Harry began to sob aloud and that, together with Tom's low and continuous groaning, sent Sean's mind racing. How could he ever have hated them? The enemy had been vanquished – they were licking their wounds, crying aloud, clamouring for mercy.

'I'll have to tell the police,' wept Harry.

'Why?' Sean asked him, calmly, reasonably. 'We could say Tom was doing an experiment which went wrong.'

'At this hour of the morning?'

'Why not?' said Mum. 'You don't want Tom in trouble, do you?'

'Don't tell, Dad,' sobbed Tom. 'Please don't tell.'

Harry continued to sob. 'We'd better get the story straight then,' he wept.

They were just finalising the details when Sean heard the by now familiar sound of a siren.

Harry travelled in the ambulance with Tom, leaving Sean and his mother to clean up.

'Tom must have hated me an awful lot to do that,' he told her, but then Sean remembered how he had half-strangled his stepbrother only yesterday yet had been dubbed a hero. Tom must have been devastated at not getting a mountain bike first, and being asked to choose the colour must have really rubbed salt into the wound. No wonder he had chosen red – for rage. Would he ever understand why his father had made such a fatal mistake? All because he wanted to get 'in' with his stepson?

'By the way,' said Mum as they walked back into the kitchen. 'I've got some news. Your dad phoned late last night when you were in bed. He's made a decision. I was keeping it back as a surprise for you at breakfast.'

'What is it?' yelled Sean, suddenly beside himself with anxiety. 'Is he getting married or going abroad or –'

'He's going to move back here and get a flat and a new job.'

Sean could hardly believe what she had just said. 'You're not –'

'Joking? Why should I be joking about such an important decision? He wants to be near you.'

'You're not going to get together again and –' He couldn't get the words out.

'No,' said Mum firmly. 'You know that's not going to happen, but it's going to be easier for you, isn't it?'

'That's fantastic. That's *much* better than any mountain bike.'

'Better not let Harry hear you say that.'

'I'm sorry about the way I've treated him...and Tom.'

'Maybe with your dad coming to live nearby –' She broke off. 'Why don't you take the day off school?'

Sean gazed at his mother as if she had just taken leave of her senses.

'We could go to the hospital and see how Tom's getting on.' She gazed at him searchingly. 'You're not going to hold it against Tom? I mean, I know what he did was a terrible thing, but surely he's suffering enough?'

Sean nodded. He reckoned he was.

*

Tom lay on his back in the hospital bed, his hands in plastic sleeves. Harry had gone to join Mum in the waiting room, leaving the two of them alone together.

'I'm sorry I wrecked your new bike.' Tom looked grey and drawn and Sean knew that he was still in great pain.

'I'm sorry I tried to strangle you.'

'I hear your dad's coming back to live round here.'

'Yeah.'

'That'll be good.'

'I've been missing him.'

There was a short, awkward silence.

Then Sean said, 'I'm going to try and get on better with Harry.'

'Maybe he prefers you to me.' Tom sounded his old, edgy self.

'No chance.'

'Why not?'

'Didn't he tell you what he's getting you for your birthday?'

'He said I was having a surprise. It's probably some rotten old clothes or something.'

Suddenly Sean realised that Harry had left it to him to tell Tom what the surprise was. That seemed more than generous – perhaps to both of them.

'It's a mountain bike.'

Tom gazed at Sean in amazement. 'Why didn't he tell me?'

'Maybe he believes in surprises.'

'If I'd known, I wouldn't have burnt down the shed,' muttered Tom, and they gazed at each other in confusion.

'I think he hoped we'd go mountain biking together,' said Sean.

'That wouldn't have been a bad idea.'

'I'm going to do a newspaper round. Then I can afford a new bike. In time.'

'I'll give you mine.'

Sean shook his head. 'I don't want you to do that. But there is something else I'd like.'

'What's that?'

'Us to be mates.'

'I'll try,' Tom said.

'So will I.'

Sean decided to walk home from the hospital. The morning was overcast with a light drizzle but he hardly noticed. He was more aware of the fact that all his old anger seemed to have left him.

A police car drew up beside him and PC Warren's head emerged. 'Couple of lads being stupid with their science homework last night,' he said. 'We were informed and I recognised the address.'

Sean nodded, trying not to show any expression or emotion.

'Three fires in three days,' persisted PC Warren. 'And you're around every time. It must be a record.'

Suddenly Sean was swept with terror. 'I didn't start them.'

'I didn't say you did.'

'I *know* I didn't.'

'Don't be so defensive, Sean,' said PC Warren. 'You're worrying about nothing.'

'Nothing?'

'Just a few coincidences, that's all. Stop worrying. By the way, that vagrant now claims he *didn't* set the wood alight. We're not taking the case any further, largely because he's got a drink problem, so his memory isn't quite what it should be.'

Sean suddenly felt very cold, but as he gazed at PC Warren he sensed that he was afraid too.

'So many coincidences could make you think

too much and look for things that probably don't exist.'

Sean nodded, his convictions reinforced.

'Take care of yourself then,' replied PC Warren, and he drove away.

When he got home, Mum didn't answer his call, but hearing movement above him he quietly climbed the stairs. He listened at the bedroom door but there was a deep, deep silence. Then Sean heard the sound of crying coming from his own room.

Sean went in to find his mother sitting on his bed, gazing miserably down at the duvet.

'What's the matter?' he asked cautiously. But she only looked away.

Then Sean saw that more of his duvet had been singed and he felt the raw fear moving inside him again.

'How did that happen?' he whispered.

'What?' She gazed up at him as if she hadn't even heard him come into the room. 'Oh that? The iron was too hot. It doesn't look too bad, does it? I've done it before. I should have told you but I felt such a fool.'

Sean breathed a sigh of relief. Then he wondered why he could have been stupid enough to think the patch was spreading.

'Why were you crying?' he tried again.

'I was worrying about you all. Wondering how you were going to get along.'

'We're going to try,' said Sean. 'That's all we can do.'

Sean waited for his mum to leave, then pulled his diary out from under the bed and read the inscription in the front again. This time, because his father was going to live nearby, the words didn't hurt so much.

He found a pen and began to write.

I still don't know how so many fires have happened. I can't list them again or I'll go crazy. But at least I'm sure of one thing. I didn't start any of them. I couldn't have done and I'm really confident about that.

Now that Dad's coming home I know it's all going to be different. We'll be friends again. We'll do things together, start running again. And even if Harry and Tom are still around, getting up my nose, life is going to be better. Life is going to be great.

All those fires were just coincidences. They can all be explained, like with the duvet. Mum did the singeing. Not me.

16

Sean had never felt so happy as he walked to school next morning. He was tired but also overjoyed, and felt a sense of freedom. Dad coming home, making up with Tom, a better relationship with Mum and maybe even a new beginning with Harry. Things were definitely looking up.

Suddenly Sean's foot slipped and he skidded, almost falling but just managing to save himself in time. Gazing back he saw a long smear of dirt on the pavement and realised he had stepped in some dog muck and his shoe was covered in the stuff.

Suddenly the gloss went off the day and as Sean went to the kerb to try to scrape the muck off his shoe the rain began.

Sean's positive thoughts about his new future suddenly disappeared into a haze of temper which flared up further when some of his schoolmates passed him on their bikes, sending a sheet of water over him. Sean yelled at them, shaking his fist. Why did the day have to start like this? He'd lost his temper and he hadn't even got to school yet.

He wiped his filthy trousers as best he could and resumed his journey, swearing to himself, his temper boiling over. Aware that he was now late, he began to jog along the pavement, angry thoughts pounding through his head in time with every step.

Suddenly he heard the sound of glass shattering, but he didn't turn back to look. Whatever it was, it had nothing to do with him. Desperately he tried to cling on to the optimism he had felt earlier, as behind him, there was a sudden flash. Flames leapt through the windows of the newsagents, and the customers ran into the street, but Sean jogged on without looking back.

As he approached the school gates, Sean heard sirens and went cold inside.